Praise For When Elsa Sang The Blues

"**Deeply** humane collection about loss, yearning, and fleeting connections. Bogaty...craft[s] stories where it hurts to feel this deeply, but it's also what makes his characters human."
—*Publishers Weekly Booklife Reviews* **Editor's Pick**

"**Bittersweet** and complicated tales of the heart. ...the author's characters collide in passion... Bogaty has perfected the open-ended conclusion, which, like a photograph, leaves things open to interpretation."
—*Kirkus Reviews* **Our Verdict: Get It**

"**The** short story collection *When Elsa Sang The Blues* ruminates on complex personal relations with flair. Whimsical themes and dreamy language."
—*Foreword Clarion Reviews*

Also By Lewis Bogaty: Loves And Entanglements

Thirteen moving stories of men and women caught in emotions
they struggle to understand and control.

———◦———

"**A**n impressively thoughtful and compelling collection of
tales."
—*Kirkus Reviews* **Our Verdict: Get It**

"**B**ogaty has truly outdone himself with his vivid storytelling
and impeccable attention to detail."
—*Midwest Book Review*

"**A** rare short story collection that manages to be a page-turner
from one story to the next...An intense collection of characters in emotional tumult...these stories are visceral and subtly
brilliant. A masterclass in storytelling structure and execution."
—*SPR*

When Elsa Sang The Blues
Blues

Stories

Lewis Bogaty

Published by One Marble Desk Publishing.
Published and printed in the United States of America

ISBN 979-8-9884054-3-6 paperback
ISBN 979-8-9884054-4-3 hardcover
ISBN 979-8-9884054-5-0 e-book

Cover Photo, "Shadow On The Building Wall," By The Author

Several of the stories in this collection were previously published in magazines in slightly different forms:
"In Saint-Rémy And Auvers" originally appeared in *Black River Review*.
"The Country House" originally appeared in *Wind Magazine*.
"The Slugger And Henry Joraleman" originally appeared in *Fan Magazine*.
"Gridlock" originally appeared in *Descant*.

For My Parents, Harry and Helene:
Always eager to read my work, wise in their comments, and
unfailingly encouraging.

Contents

Preface

In *When Elsa Sang The Blues*, as in my first collection, *Loves And Entanglements*, I have selected stories written over many years. The earliest story here was written in 1981 and the most recent in 2022. The stories reflect their times. Time-related attitudes and details have not been altered.

I thought it would be interesting to include both "But Not For Me" and "Nicky And Cat: A Romance" in the collection because the two stories, written over thirty years apart, are different takes on essentially the same drama.

Putting together this collection, rereading stories written over such a wide arc of time, has led me, not surprisingly, to reflect on time's passage. "Time," Hotspur says in *Henry IV Part 1*, "must have a stop." And so in art, in fiction, it does. Stories freeze and clarify the flux of society's dizzying and relentless motion, freeze moments in lives, as Keats' Grecian urn famously shows us, and make them eternal. A writer hopes, I hope, when writing fiction, that the moments I am stopping and holding up to view capture an essence that transcends time.

For me, at least, Elsa transcends time, is eternal. As I sit here writing this preface, I find myself smiling anew as I hear her in my head, banging on the piano keys and belting out those hot, hot, dirty songs, to raucous whoops and inebriated guffaws and mellow smiles of quiet appreciation.

But Not For Me

G RACIELA SHAW AND JAKE Simon had spent a romantic Saturday night at his apartment in a brownstone off Riverside Drive in New York City. Still awake at dawn, they decided to walk along the Hudson River while the July day was cool. She threw on one of his tee shirts, which hung loosely off her shoulders, and a pair of his sweat pants with the legs rolled up. "Ragamuffin," he called her. "Stubble face," she responded. They walked, holding hands, in the golden light. When their sleepiness at last overcame them, they lay down together on the grass in Riverside Park and quickly drifted off.

A mother calling to her child to stop running woke them up close to one o'clock in the afternoon. Jake's left arm was numb. Graciela had ended up lying sprawled on top of him. As he saw her wake up he was filled with the joy her disheveled sight in the morning always gave him, maybe even a little more so because they were outdoors along the river. At first she looked confused. Then she abruptly sat up, wiped her mouth on her sleeve and peered around her, a look of shock on her face.

Their spot, where they had been alone at five a.m., was now teeming with an array of pastel blankets and bright summer clothes. Jake saw that many nearby people were watching them with curiosity. Someone somewhere clapped, and then quite a few people started smiling, and clapping, until it became a chorus of applause. Jake smiled and waved, gave a little half bow, but Graciela was mortified. He was surprised. While she was certainly private — quiet-spoken, watchful, and cerebral, not someone he would ever expect to be the life of a party — he hadn't thought of her as particularly shy.

Even when the people stopped clapping and looked away, she refused to kiss him, and was anxious to go. When he didn't move fast enough, she stood up and started walking away by herself. He caught up. They walked in silence.

Back at his apartment she disappeared into the bathroom.

"I have to go too," he said.

"In a minute."

"I would have been much faster. You should have let me go first."

"Well you weren't quick enough, were you?"

When she came out she started collecting her things. "I have to go."

"What's wrong?"

"Nothing." She gave her mop of frizzy black hair a quick shake of emphasis.

"Nothing?"

She didn't respond.

He took her by the shoulders and looked down into her India-ink eyes. They stared at each other for seconds. "I have to go," she said. "I was supposed to have lunch with my parents. I told them I would be there at noon. Then last night I left a message changing it to three. My mother will be pissed enough at that. Now I'll never get to Tenafly even close to that. She'll be furious."

He continued to look at her. "What did I do? I don't under-stand."

"I told you. I told my mother..."

"Yeah, but something's wrong. Why won't you tell me?"

She looked around, eyed the big chair in which they had spent much of the night. But she didn't sit. When she looked back up at him, she said simply, "Life isn't a song."

"What?"

"I don't know, nothing."

"I don't get what happened."

"I just realized, once summer started, things have gotten so..." She searched for a word, "...so intense, I don't know, I've, we've, it's like we're in a fantasy cocoon. This isn't real life. Actually, I didn't just realize; it has been on my mind for a while."

"What isn't? What has?"

"Us. This." She frowned up at him with exasperation on her face. "People's lives aren't like this. Nothing is this perfect. It's not real. It's like an idyll."

"Listen to what you said, how absurd it is. You admit our time together is 'perfect,' then say people can't be that happy, so something is wrong."

"School is going to be starting in another few weeks. I'm going to be really busy. I have a really heavy load of hard classes this semester, and two jobs and obligations."

"You think I'm not busy now at work?"

"Do you want to come home with me, right now!"

He gave her a wry look. "Can I take a shower first? I have to be at my best to impress the old codger."

"Really funny."

"All right. Yes. I've never been against it. It's a good idea. You'll stop obsessing on it."

She sighed. "You know that isn't happening. My mother would freak out. Not to mention the reason; the unassailable fact."

"What fact? My indubitable whiteness?"

"What fact," she mimicked him with impatience. "That you are my father's age. Can you come to grips with that, please. Face it!"

"No I won't. It is a completely meaningless statement. First of all, I am not actually your father's age. So much for 'unassailable' facts." He nodded his head to punctuate the point.

"You're splitting hairs."

"And your father had you when he was barely eighteen. Do the math."

"I've done the math. It still blows me away. I can't help it. You know this can't work. We're in different places. You want something I'm not ready for yet. I'm just starting to experience things; I have so many plans. You think you'd be happy partying with my friends? I'm too young to — to what? Settle down? Move to the suburbs? What exactly do you want from me?"

"Who said anything about the suburbs? I live here."

She scowled at him.

"I just want to be with you." He trailed off.

"Look, could we talk in a few days? I need to think. Last night, and then all those people watching us. I have to get my bearings. I'll call you."

"What can I say?"

"Nothing. I have to go." And she did.

⸺◆⸺

He would have liked to think he was love sick, but it was a bad cold that hit him the next morning. At first, he was sure it was Covid. He rummaged through his pile of free tests, all expired. Finding one that was barely a month beyond expiration, he discovered that he did not have Covid. So he went to the office, announcing defensively to each frown he encountered that he had tested himself.

"It does not matter," a fellow lawyer in his group said angrily. "If you are sick, go the fuck home." She stood glaring at him, pulling a mask out of her jacket pocket. He did go home, and felt worse and worse as the day went on. By Tuesday he had a real fever, had lost his voice, could barely lift himself out of bed. Maybe it was the flu.

When the phone rang, her, he answered it with an indescribably obscene sound.

"I'm sorry, I must have the wrong number."

"Uuuh ts eeee. Eee." But she was gone. Incomprehensible; how could she think she had a wrong number when she pressed his name on her phone. She called a second time while he was in the bathroom.

He listened to her message with trepidation: Just, "Call me." He heard no warmth in her voice; instead a tension. He felt a chill that was more than his fever. He both wanted to put off the conversation and have it. He was left with frustration that he could not call her back without her hanging up on him. He didn't want to text. He wanted to hear her voice. He found himself pacing the room. He felt so weak suddenly that he lay down on the bed and fell asleep in spite of himself.

She didn't call again. Why would she?

He waited until evening, drinking tea, but it became clear his voice was not coming back. He texted her. "I'm sick."

Later, while he was lying in bed watching the news, she called.

"Huuh ohh."

"Oh my God," she said. He heard her lighting a cigarette. He hated that she smoked. He heard her blow out the smoke slowly, as if considering the situation. "What's wrong with you?" she said.

"Ick."

"Yeah, I think so. Did you test yourself?"

"Uhh. Not Covid."

"Glad to hear that! Do you need anything?"

"Just you," was what he wanted to say, but he remained silent.

"Are you drinking plenty? Do you have any chicken soup?"

"Ohh."

"Is that 'No'?"

"Uh."

After a moment's silence she said, "I'm coming over." She hung up without waiting for a response. While he was longing to see her, he dreaded what she planned to say.

He was just so sleepy. He unbolted all his door locks, took out his winter coat and threw it on, shivering. He walked down the stairs carefully and opened the front door just enough to stick a folded piece of someone's junk mail in the jamb to prevent the door from closing all the way. He hoped the building's five other tenants were already in for the night. He hoped she would notice that the door was open and not ring. He hoped a lot of things.

He wore himself out climbing back up the stairs. He lay down in bed and was soon asleep. When he awoke in the morning she was asleep beside him. He felt gratitude and relief that quite literally took whatever breath he had away. His coughing woke her up.

She raised herself and squinted at him through puffy eyes. With a frown of concern, she examined him, then leaned over and brushed his hair off his forehead with her fingers. She gazed at him, shaking her head. "You look like shit."

"Anks."

She felt his forehead, then sighed. "I can't tell. I guess Florence N. I'm not. Do you have a fever?"

He nodded. "Did anyway," he tried unsuccessfully to say.

"How much?"

He put up ten fingers twice, then one finger, then pointed straight ahead, then two.

"A hundred and one point two." she said.

He nodded and smiled. Not everyone would have gotten that immediately.

She shook her head slowly. "You poor baby." He made a pouting face, feeling so happy. She bent down to kiss him, but he turned his head away. "On't. Oooll atch it."

She kissed him anyway, easing her tongue into his resisting mouth. Then she lay back down with her head on his chest.

She stayed with him the whole week, mothering him those first few days. Every so often he noticed her looking off into space, thinking. She would catch herself and give him a little smile. It scared him. By late in the week, as his symptoms lessened just a bit, she caught whatever it was he had. Limp and drained and feverish though he still felt, he now mothered her.

She got slammed with a chest cough and a runny nose that would not stop long enough for her to snatch a tissue out of the box. Her greasy, pungent-smelling hair hung in limp clumps. Her bloodshot eyes were puffy, her swollen nose bright red, with the skin all around it raw and flaking. She no longer looked off in space wondering what to do about the future. She had not said a word about her reason for calling him. Awful as he felt for her misery, he felt relief at that, at least.

They were listening to music a little. He'd put a George Gershwin album on. As a song played, he found himself looking off into space.

"That's kind of sad," she said. He looked at her. "Those words," she explained.

"Yeah."

"What's that song called?"

"I think, 'But Not For Me.'"

He felt so anxious then that he pulled her tight so they were not looking at each other.

The humidity of this July did not quit. They had turned the air conditioner off because Graciela was having bouts of chills. They lay in bed together, both feverish, both enervated. They talked idly, more croaked than talked, too lethargic now even to watch a movie or listen to music. He had forced himself up to shave because his scratchy face was hurting her inflamed skin when they got close. The heavy air coated them with sweat as they hunkered under the blanket hot and cold at the same time, dozing on and off into hallucinatory dreams.

He was awake just now, looking at the streak of sunlight dappling the books in the bookcase, slowly making its way along the spines as the minutes passed. With the window open, he could hear the distant sounds of voices on the street below. It was the sound of sick days in his bedroom in his parent's home long ago.

She had had a rough morning. Summer colds are the worst, Jake thought, as he watched her finally doze. He was restraining himself with great difficulty from rousing her, impatient to have her back with him.

At last, she woke, seemingly from a dream, and looked disoriented. When she saw him, leaning on his elbow watching her, she smiled. She reached up and pulled his head down, kissed him carefully, to minimize the pain to her inflamed skin.

Sleep had brought her a burst of energy. She started pulling off his underpants with one hand and he said, "You don't have your thing in." She was blowing her nose with a tissue in the other hand and didn't respond. "Aren't you going to put it in?" he asked, as she slid her own panties down.

She climbed on top of him, coughing. Her nose started to run again as they looked at each other. He licked the new stream away, tasting the saltiness.

"Uh uv ouh," she croaked. And then she tried it again, soundlessly mouthing the words. It was such an unexpected answer to his question of why she had called him. He had never heard words that relieved and excited him more. He kissed her very gently.

"Umm intuh ee," she said.

"You didn't put the thing in," he reminded her.

Her mouth was against his, her breath thick and hot, her skin fevered. "Come into me," she said again, so softly all he could really hear was the intensity in her voice.

Her mouth was open, panting as she tried to get air. Her insistence was palpable.

His hands clenched against her back, bunching her skin tight. Her words made him wildly excited and then he spoke in a whisper. "What are you saying? Do you want me to make a baby in you?" She made an inarticulate sound in her throat, and pulled his resisting body up to her.

"Do you?" he asked. His heart pounded against his chest, or was it hers he felt? They stared at each other wide-eyed, as if asking each other, "What are we doing?" She took hold of his cock and without taking her eyes from his, maneuvered it against her.

His brown eyes and her black ones locked as if they would never break away. He opened his mouth, at first unable to get words out. She watched him, panting, curious.

"If we make it, we keep it," he said.

She didn't respond. Just kept looking at him. "I love you," she said again. Abruptly, he felt her warm insides surrounding and squeezing him. She let out a howling cry as he felt her start to come and then a grunt of frustration as he mustered every ounce of sense and willpower he possessed to pull out of her and come on her stomach. She frantically pushed his head down between her legs. She came and came, her body vibrating against his mouth. This, he thought, was 'like never before.' When she finally relaxed with an exhausted half-cough half-groan, he hoisted himself up to again look into her dark eyes. "Graciela," he said. "I love you beyond words. Do you understand how much? Do you?"

They were both still breathing hard, and her nose was running. Her searching eyes roamed his features.

She blew her nose.

They flopped down in a heap, and lay together wordlessly for a long time. His head rested on her chest. He listened to the rhythmic beating of her heart, and to her paroxysms of coughing that bounced his head around. He tried to fathom what had transpired, while she tossed tissue after soggy tissue in the general direction of the trash basket.

And then, next morning, the fever broke.

He awoke feeling glorious. The open windows brought in the scent of a beautiful cool summer day as sun streamed across the bed. Graciela was not beside him. He got up and went to make coffee. "Graciela, you in the bathroom?" he called as he filled two cups. The smell of the coffee was intoxicating. But she didn't answer. "Graciela?"

He walked to the bathroom, but she wasn't there. He opened his front door and looked in the hallway, which he knew made no sense, but he was confused. He was frowning as he walked back in. Then he saw the note, in her careful, beautiful printing, sitting on the cushion of the battered living room chair they enjoyed sharing though it was too small for the two of them: "I need to take a break. I'll call you in a couple of weeks." And an incongruous, "Feel better." And after that it said, "Love, G." It did say that.

He waited patiently. Impatiently, actually. But he didn't call her. At least not the first week. Not the second week either. Then with his hands shaking, he did call her. She didn't answer. He left no message. Instead, he texted her. She did not respond. As two weeks became three and then four, he left several gentle reminders of his existence each week. The university was back in session now. He knew she must be very busy. So he waited. In his gut... in his heart... in his soul.... He dismissed those words. In his *brain*, he knew her silence meant she was gone. In those other places, he was sure that could not be true.

It was drizzling out, the tops of buildings fading into fog, the asphalt glittery with red and yellowish white oil streaks. He was restless, so he was walking up to the Hungarian Pastry Shop to sit and read for a while. It was where he had met her all those months ago. Broadway was filled with students, teenagers most of them it seemed.

He almost didn't see her among the throng, in front of Tom's, walking toward him — it was her graceful, controlled but effortless walk that caught his eye. She wore jeans with manufactured rips in them, and an orange tank top, and ballet slippers. He stopped so abruptly a woman walking behind him had to apologize for banging her umbrella into him.

Graciela was arm in arm with a short skinny kid with a ludicrous beard on his face, a backward baseball cap on his head, and a tee shirt of some rap group Jake had never heard of, nor wanted to hear of. They shared a laugh about something. Eventually she saw Jake and she slowed down. The bearded twerp glanced over at her as she stopped walking. Her eyes met Jake's for an endless moment. Her no-longer-laughing face was unreadable. Their whole July, and then all their months before, played through his head as he stared at her delicate body, her black hair matted by the rain. His gaze returned to her unwavering eyes. She mouthed, "I'm sorry," as her companion pulled her forward.

Talya, And Dolly's Comb

TALYA'S STEP LOSES ITS after-school spring as she approaches her apartment and remembers it is Tuesday. "I'm home, Tetey," she says as she opens the door and tiptoes in.

Talya dreads Tuesdays when her mother works late and she is alone with Tetey from three o'clock until nine o'clock. Scooting into the bedroom, she drops her school case in the corner. She slips off her uniform, a blue skirt hemmed just above the knees, white blouse with wide, round collars, and a sweater. Shivering in the icy cold bedroom, she hurries into pants and a warm shirt. She reaches for her doll and hugs it as she walks into the kitchen where she finds Tetey mopping the stone floor in her loose-fitting, faded, paisley dress. The ankle-length dress sways and ripples as she mops. Tetey does not acknowledge Talya, which is a relief.

The coal stove provides the only heat in the apartment. Talya picks the chair closest to the stove, and sits down at the big wooden table, happy to be warm. She has a conversation with Dolly as she combs its blond hair with Dolly's own tiny pink comb. The comb is so small it fits inside Talya's little palm. "Do you like when I comb it to the side this way, Dolly?"

Dolly's blue eyes blink open and closed. "No Talya, I want it pulled back like Tetey's," Dolly answers in a squeaky voice.

Tetey's ancient eyes shoot a look at Talya as she hears her name. Talya doesn't notice. She tunes Tetey out as much as she can. Tetey's hair is always pulled back under a kerchief tied behind with a bow. Gray strands fly out in all directions from under the kerchief. Talya shakes her head at Dolly and makes a face. "I think it's much better this way Dolly. Mommy will like it a lot when she comes home."

"If you think so, Talya," Dolly squeaks.

"You're such a pretty girl, Dolly. I tell you just like Mommy always tells me I am."

"Pretty. Hah." Tetey's wrinkled face creases in a lurid mask, exposing her mostly toothless mouth. "Mongolian bastard," she mutters. She is bent over the mop, rubbing hard at the floor. Then she suddenly stands her skeletal body erect, points a bony finger at Talya. "Get out of my way. Move, faster, faster."

Dolly falls as Talya jumps up. She wants to reach down for Dolly, but she doesn't dare. She has never understood why Tetey does not seem to like her. Mommy's friends all like her.

When Mommy invited her Tatar friends over for tea on Sunday, Talya was telling them all about school. They were asking her questions about her classes and teacher and were very interested in what she was explaining to them while Mommy was preparing the tea. They called her Talyushka Matur, her father's endearment for her. Then Tetey chased her away, telling her to go in the bedroom and leave the women alone. "What are you doing here," she scolded, shooing Talya away with her hands.

The women looked at each other. Talya heard one woman say to the other, "How is it possible that Tetey is treating this child in this way. Talya is so respectful and obliging."

"And sweet," says another, giving Tetey a disapproving look.

"It is so nice to see her chattering away. She is usually so shy and quiet."

With Talya now, Tetey is saying, "I step on your miserable doll." She stands poised with her foot in the air. "Should I?"

"No please, Tetey."

"You are cursed, do you know that?"

"No I'm not. Mommy says I am a very sweet girl. The ladies say that too."

"You disgust me. You are a Mongolian bastard. You were born bad. Do you know what will become of you?"

Tears start to run down Talya's face and she snatches Dolly from the floor and runs into the cold bedroom. Tetey mutters behind her in the kitchen. Talya shuts the door and climbs onto the bed, burrows under the covers, shivering. She starts to sob.

Why did they have to come to Turkey? Her mother has told her the Tatars are Turkic people, so when they had to leave Inner Mongolia, Turkey allowed them to come. She doesn't like Turkey. The people are not friendly. Sometimes walking down the block with her friend, men admonish them for speaking Tatar instead of Turkish. She is learning Turkish fairly quickly, because the two languages are so similar.

She misses Daddy so much. In the frigid early Mongolian mornings, Talya would sit on the stove, which was still warm from the day before, and drink soup while Daddy told her stories. She comforts herself now by thinking about how proud and happy she felt on the days when his friends, the doctors, all came to their house to drink and sing songs of the land and the horses and the trees and sky. Daddy was a doctor. A surgeon. Mommy was a doctor then too, an opthom something, an eye doctor. But Mommy said she would have had to go to school for two years here to be allowed to be a doctor. She did not have the money. She is working at the American air base in the store called PX.

She says she is lucky to have gotten this job because she knows English. The Americans pay much more than the Turks.

Talya always sat on daddy's lap while the doctors smoked and drank and sang songs. They told her what an adorable little girl she was. Daddy smiled and kissed her on the neck and bounced her on his knee and told her that she was his princess and Mommy was his queen and he adored them both. "Talyushka Matur," he would say, "Do you know how much I love love love you?"

Sometimes the doctors did not sing. They talked seriously. They talked in quiet voices about the communists. Life was becoming more and more dangerous. And then one day Mommy said many of the Tatars were coming here, to Ankara, Turkey. Mommy's friends all told Talya she would love it. They would have running water in their house in this new land. Even a bathroom inside the house. And no cows and horses outside. Talya liked petting the horse that the neighbor kept in a lean-to near the outhouse in their backyard, so that did not make her want to leave.

They left Hailar in Inner Mongolia together, Mommy and Daddy and Talya. Mommy warned her it would be a very, very long trip, a big adventure. They would take a train from Hailar nearly at the Siberian border to Harbin, and from Harbin another train all the way through China to Tientsin, and then a ship to Hong Kong where they would board an airplane to India. Riding on the ship through the water would be so much fun, she told Talya. And flying through the clouds, imagine that. From India they would take another airplane to Istanbul, and from Istanbul a bus to Ankara where they would join Aunt Kamila and live with her until they found an apartment. The timing of their arrival worked out very conveniently, Sevim said. Aunt Kamila's children were now grown and she no longer needed her wonderful nanny, Tetey, to take care of them. She would pass Tetey on to them.

"Come in for dinner, Talya," Tetey calls.

Talya realizes she is very hungry. She returns to the kitchen, giving Tetey a quick glance. She is standing at the stove stirring the contents of the pan. Talya sits down, happy for the heat of the stove, her mouth watering with the smell of peremec frying. Talya loves the twists of dough stuffed with meat. Tetey brings two plates and sits down across from her. They eat in silence, listening to the music playing on the radio. "May I have more please?" Talya asks. Tetey takes her plate and fills it. They continue to eat, lost in their own thoughts.

On days when Tetey feels like talking, she tells Talya and her mother about war in Russia many years before, when the women picked rotting food out of the garbage dump to eat. "We were starving," she likes to say, setting her jaw and looking proud. "Do you know what it is to be hungry?" she demands of Talya. "No, you do not. I could not even make milk for my baby, and he starved. One morning, he was dead in my arms." One day when she repeats this story she adds, "I'm glad he died. It was better that way."

"No," Talya's mother protests. "No."

"Yes." Tetey nods her head. "Yes."

After eating, Talya returns to the bedroom and Dolly, relieved to be alone again. Soon enough, she falls asleep and is awakened by the door squeaking open. Her mother stands in the doorway beaming. It is dark out now, and the room light is off. But Talya can just make her out. She is a large, round, soft woman, with a pretty face.

"Mommy."

When Sevim sees that Talya is awake, she comes running to the bed, still wearing her fur coat, with open arms flapping, and making a whirring sound in her throat that starts Talya laughing. She wraps Talya up and rolls over with her. "My darling girl. Did you have a wonderful day? I missed you all day, do you know that? All day long. Tell me about school. Why are you in this cold room instead of in the toasty warm kitchen? Come, let's go inside. You sit with me while I eat the dinner Tetey kept warm for me." She carries Talya into the kitchen. "Oh my big girl. You're getting too heavy for Mommy to carry. Six years old. I can hardly believe it. Can you, Tetey? Talya, 1957 minus 1951 is how much? Seven minus one equals?"

"Six," Talya shouts out.

"That is correct! She's so smart, isn't she Tetey? How was my girl today, Tetey? Was she a good girl?"

"Oh yes, good girl. Very good girl." Tetey is filling a plate with food.

"Oh boy, Talya," Sevim says, "Peremec, our favorite. Was it delicious?"

Talya nods, and reaches for a twist of dough.

"Talya, don't eat from your mother's plate," Tetey says.

Sevim laughs. "You still a hungry girl, my love?"

"No," Talya says, with a grin, "but I want more anyway."

Sevim pats her head. "Tetey, bring another plate over for her."

Tetey nods and fills a plate.

Talya and Sevim sit down and eat together. Talya tells her about her day at school. Not quite all. She does not tell her about Mert. Mert is a little boy, no bigger than Talya, with red hair and freckles. He is not nice to Talya.

Last year, in Kindergarten, Talya loved her teacher, Ceyda. When she saw Mert bothering Talya, she quickly shooed him away. Ceyda was pretty and sweet, and she always had a big smile for Talya. Most of the Tatars lived in a different part of town. All the children in Talya's class were Turkish. But

Ceyda made Talya feel very comfortable. Much of Talya's time in Kindergarten was spent learning Turkish, and Ceyda made it easy for her. The girls in the class said that Talya was the teacher's pet. Some of the boys teased her about it.

Talya's mother often invited her friends over for tea, so Talya thought it would be the proper thing to do one day at the end of class to invite Ceyda over for tea. She was Talya's friend, and the apartment building was right behind the school, so what could be more natural than to have her teacher stop by? When she offered the invitation, Ceyda hesitated. Talya implored her, "Please, Please, Please! Ceyda ogretmenim, Ceyda my teacher." She felt as if she were going to start crying if Ceyda said no. Ceyda saw her disappointment. She gave a little smile, thought for a moment, and said she would love to come.

Talya was very excited as Ceyda and her friend, one of the other teachers, walked with her to the small building with four apartments. Talya in her uniform skipped along between them as each held her by a hand. She pointed out her apartment with enthusiasm. When they walked in, Tetey squinted at the happily laughing women with confusion, and then at Talya with displeasure. What did she think she was doing, the look said. How dare you bring people here? You are a child. Who are you to bring people to the house? Tetey did not offer the teachers tea, which was very discourteous, and after looking around for a few minutes, they said goodbye to Talya and left.

Talya's first grade teacher, Fatime is stern and severe. She does not mistreat the children, but she is not warm. Talya thinks of her as sour and gray. She wears gray suits and has gray hair. One day in the cafeteria, during lunch, Talya leaves her vegetable, okra, on the plate. Fatime is patrolling between the tables and Talya hears her admonishing other children to eat their okra. She is sure she can not eat the slimy stuff. Soon, though, Fatime stops in front of Talya.

"Talya, you must eat your vegetable. You want to grow to be a strong girl, don't you?"

"I really really really really can't. Please don't make me."

"Try one bite dear."

Talya forces herself to put a forkful in her mouth. It feels oozy and squishy on her tongue and she has all she can do to keep from spitting it out. She chews as fast as she can, feeling herself start to gag, and gulps it down.

"Good girl." Fatime moves on, looking for other vegetable shirkers.

As Talya is vowing to herself that she will never ever eat okra again, Mert sneaks up behind her, and pulls one of her braided pigtails.

"Stop," she says.

"Eat your okra, Talya," he mimics the teacher, making a retching sound in Talya's ear. "You have funny looking eyes." He reaches around and pinches her stomach. Talya cries out, but he is gone before she can turn."

Talya despises Mert. He bothers her every day. He always manages to be right behind her in line, when they walk to recess, standing too close to her. When she can feel his breath on her neck, she knows that he is about to pull her pigtails. Sometimes he says, "Choo, Choo," when he pulls, as if he is pulling a train whistle. Sometimes he just makes fun of her eyes. Some of the other boys make fun of her eyes too.

Talya does not understand what is wrong with her eyes. At home she often stares at her eyes in the mirror. Her eyes look perfectly normal to her. She studies them and studies them, but she just does not see anything funny about her eyes. She watches Tetey scrub the clothes in the sink against a wash board and take them out to the courtyard to hang on the line to dry. She tries to examine Tetey's eyes as she passes by, but they are tiny and lost in the wrinkles of her face.

At eleven-thirty each morning, right before lunch, Talya's assignment is to practice writing in Turkish for half an hour. She may write about whatever she wishes. Fatime has explained to her that this is not an assignment that must be turned in. Nobody will look at it. She should not worry about grammar or spelling. She should just practice putting her thoughts into Turkish words. Fatime suggests writing about her journey to Turkey or about foods she likes or things she does with her friends. She has made several friends. A girl in the class named Pinar is her best friend, but she does not have anything to write about Pinar. She tries writing about the other things the teacher suggested, but her pencil always wants to write about the same thing. It writes down whatever Tetey has said to her the night before. Writing the words down makes her feel relief. It is as if when the words come out of the pencil and onto the page they are no longer pressing down on her heart. She feels light. She can breathe. Each day she looks forward to filling the pages, and then enjoying her lunch.

"You are a bad person," she writes. "Do you know what the soul is? You need to have a soul to go to heaven and you were born without one." "You are not a good Muslim. You do not pray. You and your mother both." Across the street from their apartment, a vast field of wheat sprawls. At the far end of the field, all alone in the empty distance with nothing behind it but sky sits the Ataturk Mausoleum. Mommy says Ataturk was a good man who made Turkey a modern country, and gave women the right to vote. But that is not what Tetey tells her.

Talya writes, "When the moon is full, the ghost of Ataturk comes out from his house and walks in the field. He is coming toward you, saying 'Talya, Talya'. He is angry. He does not like little Mongolian bastards. One night, he will snatch you up and take you away. We will be rid of you." Sometimes Talya thinks she hears Ataturk walking in the field, rustling the grass. She holds tight to Mommy in the big bed where they sleep. Sometimes Talya wakes up thinking she hears the ghostly sound of Ataturk speaking, and gets frightened, but then realizes it is Tetey talking in her sleep in her bed in the kitchen.

Talya's favorite times are the moments she has with her mother. In the mornings, Talya sits as Sevim braids her black hair into two pigtails that have now grown to reach her waist. It is comforting to sit with Mommy by the stove and talk as Mommy makes her braids. In the evenings, Sevim brushes her hair. Television has not yet come to Turkey. Sevim has the radio and a record player, but they do not even have a telephone. Sevim likes to read detective stories to relax. As she sits reading and smoking, Talya sits on her lap drawing in her coloring books with her crayons.

Sometimes before bed, Sevim tells Talya stories about how her family came to be in Mongolia. Many years ago there was a war, a revolution in Russia, and the communists came to power. The communists were very bad, and killed many people. In Tatarstan, people were frightened, and many left. Many went to Inner Mongolia. Mommy's parents went to Inner Mongolia and Mommy was born there. When Mommy grew up, she met Daddy. Daddy was not a Tatar. He was Mongolian.

Daddy told Talya stories of the great warrior Genghis Khan, and the glorious Kubla Khan. She loved hearing the stories. Sometimes when Tetey is mean to her, she lies under the covers thinking about Genghis Khan, dreaming that the great Khan will come and carry Tetey away. Talya does not know what a bastard is, but she knows something is wrong with her family. Daddy lived with Mommy in Hailar, but he had another family off in the country. Talya had three half-brothers and two half-sisters in the countryside. Sometimes the oldest daughter, Begum, who was sixteen when Talya was four, came to town with her mother. One time they stopped at the house without warning and when they saw Talya, they ran at her, swinging their fists, shouting "Get out of here. Why don't you go away," hitting her with their fists. The Tatar women gathered round Talya to protect her and rushed her out of the room, hiding her until they were gone.

Tonight, Mommy is sitting smoking and reading a book near the coal stove. Talya has a pair of scissors and is talking to herself as she sits cutting Dolly's long hair.

"Look what she is doing, Sevim, look," Tetey says.

Her Mommy looks up. "What are you doing, darling? Don't you want Dolly to have hair?"

"I'm a hairdresser."

Her mother laughs. "I think you gave her a bit of an extreme hairdo, darling."

"All over the clean floor," Tetey says, clucking.

"Talya will sweep it up, right darling? That is part of the job of being a hairdresser."

"That's right, Mommy."

Talya takes a close look at Dolly's eyes. She still does not see what is different about her own eyes. "Do you like Dolly's eyes, Mommy?"

"Yes dear, they are very nice blue eyes."

"Are my eyes nice, Mommy?"

"Your eyes are big, brown, beautiful eyes. You are a beautiful little girl, do you know that?"

Dolly has a tiny hand mirror to match her comb. Talya picks it up and stares at her eyes. She does not see what is funny about her eyes. They look normal to her.

"Mommy," she says. "Are my eyes funny?"

"What, my love?"

"My eyes."

"They're lovely eyes, my darling. They are just a tiny bit different from the other children. But don't let it concern you, sweetheart. When you are older, if you want to, we can have them changed."

"Should we?"

"Only if you want to."

Talya examines her eyes in the mirror again. She still does not see what is different about them. Then she goes back to combing Dolly's hair. When she is satisfied with her work, she puts Dolly's comb in her uniform pocket. She likes to take it to school with her every day.

At school, Talya is sitting at her desk. The desks are for two children side by side, seated boy girl at each. But today Pinar is sitting next to Talya and they are conversing. Pinar is helping Talya with her Turkish, when Mert plops down at the next desk. Pinar gives him a dirty look. He sticks out his tongue at her and turns his attention to Talya. He does not say a word, but stares at her. She looks down at her book as the two girls fall silent. Mert gives Talya a kick under the table. "That is for your round Chinese face." Talya pretends she did not feel it, but her leg hurts.

Later, at recess, limping slightly, Talya sits down on a low stone wall to read a picture book. She loves to read about strange places with lions and tigers and elephants. Mert and several of his friends walk by singsonging "Ching Chong, Ching Chong" as they pass her. She glares at Mert but does not respond. She goes back to reading her book. The boys turn around and pass her again, saying "Ching Chong, Ching Chong." She ignores them.

Pinar and Talya decide to go on the swings. They are competing to see who can swing higher. Talya is winning and laughing when she feels her swing's chain suddenly tug. The swing starts to twist around in circles high in the air. Pinar screams, "Get away, you pig. Domuz."

"Dungiz," Talya shouts.

Pinar calls out, "Fatime ogretmenim, Fatime my teacher." Mert runs off as Talya manages to cling to the swing until it slows down enough for her to get off. "They are so mean," Pinar says of Mert and his friends. Talya says nothing.

Talya sits down on a bench. She starts to cry for Daddy. She wants to see him so badly. She relives her trip to Turkey. She was loving her first time on a train, though the trip was very tiring. She was happy all the way to the town of Tientsin, where everything changed. As they left the train at that station, Daddy sat down on a bench and boosted Talya on his knee and kissed her and hugged her. "Oh my darling Talyushka Matur." She saw he had tears in his eyes. He said he had something very sad to tell her.

Talya's eyes narrowed with worry.

"I can not go any further with you," he said, his voice cracking. "Although I am a Mongolian, we Mongolians are all Chinese citizens now. I am not allowed to leave the country. The communists are very strict and very dangerous."

"You can. You have to."

"My life would be in danger. You don't want anything bad to happen to Daddy, do you?"

"Then I won't go either," Talya said, her chin rising in a stubborn look.

"Oh, you must, my darling girl. It is not safe any more for foreigners to be in China. You and Mommy must go. And one day we will be together again. I promise, my Talyushka Matur."

Talya sat for a moment expressionless, but as the full import of his words dawned on her, then she began to howl. Her screams filled the train platform. She could not be controlled or consoled and she clung to her father like a vise. She could not be separated as her mother tried to walk her to the exit and her father was forced to walk along with Talya attached to him. Her mother finally pried her loose, one finger at a time, and quickly dragged her away, never having her own chance to say a proper farewell. As Talya's father stood weeping and waving, trying to smile, she continued to howl inconsolably.

A week after Mert twisted Talya's swing, the day is cold and crisp. As the class lines up for recess, Mert has managed once again to be right behind Talya. As they pass through the side door to the playground, she feels him pulling her pigtail. "Choo Choo, Ching Chong." he says and laughs.

"Don't do it again," Talya says angrily.

"What are you going to do about it, Chinese face?"

Talya does not answer. She is already looking forward to reading her picture book. She sits down on a bench and finds her place. It is very cold out, though, too cold to sit. She feels like running around to keep warm, so she stands up and looks for Pinar. Her hands are in her pockets to keep warm.

"Looking for me, funny eyes?" Mert says, coming up behind her. He gives a hard yank at her pigtails, first one then the other.

Talya cries "Owww." Her hair stings at the roots. As she hears Mert giggling, her whole body shakes. She finds herself gripping the comb in her pocket so tight that it is digging into her palm, almost piercing the skin. She swings around to face Mert and glares at his freckled face, all aglow with his success in making her angry.

Without even thinking, she pulls her hand from her pocket, raises her arm in the air, and lunges forward. She rakes the comb's points down Mert's face. She scratches him from just below his eye to his lip. As he jumps away in shock, she watches the blood drops trickle out along four long, thin streaks. Mert bellows in pain and screams "Fatime ogretmenim," and runs to the teacher.

Talya stands still, trembling with anger.

Fatime strides toward Talya, her sour face tightly knotted. "Talya," she says in a loud voice. "What did you do? What have you done to Mert?"

"She scratched me," says Mert, trailing behind, holding a handkerchief to his face. "She made me bleed. She did it. Talya did it."

"Talya?" Fatime says.

Talya says nothing. Her face has that stubborn look, her chin pulled up, her lips pressed tight. She stares at Fatime.

Fatime picks up Talya's limp hands and examines them. "It's not possible," she muses. She examines Talya's short fingernails for a long time, turns them every which way. Tetey believes a good Muslim girl should not have long nails, and she cuts Talya's especially short. "I don't see how it is possible," Fatime says to herself, running Talya's fingernails over her own wrist, pressing them down against her skin. She turns her attention to Mert, lifts his hand from his face, peers at the bleeding wounds. "I have to get you to the nurse. Tell me exactly what happened."

Mert sobs and sniffs and says, "I was walking by and she pushed me. When I turned around she scratched me with her fingernails."

Talya wants to scream out, "Liar!" but she says nothing. She stares intently at the ground.

Fatime is shaking her head back and forth, confused. She is now so engrossed in the enigma that she forgets for a moment about Mert's bleeding face. She picks up Talya's hand again. "I don't see how it is possible. Talya, step back. Let me see your uniform." Talya does not move. Fatime takes her shoulders and gently pushes her back. She bends down and examines Talya's uniform, feels with her hands at the pockets of her skirt. Talya looks up and glares into Mert's eyes. He looks away.

Fatime shakes her head yet again. "Talya," she says, "Did you do this?" Talya continues to stare at Mert, vibrating still with rage. Mert does not meet her look. Talya offers Fatime nothing.

Fatime once more runs her hand over Talya's skirt pockets. Her hand passes over Dolly's comb, but it is so small that she can not feel it through the heavy cloth. Then she reaches her hands into the deep pockets, but not far enough to touch the tiny comb at the bottom.

"I don't see that she could have done it," Fatime says more to herself than either Talya or Mert.

Talya is mute.

Fatime sighs. She turns to Mert. "Are you blaming sweet little Talya for something one of the other boys did?"

"Noooo," he wails, turning his head up to the sky.

"All right dear, all right. Come, we have to go to the infirmary and attend to your face."

Fatime leads Mert away sniffling. Talya follows them with her eyes as they crunch along the playground gravel.

Pinar, who has been watching the teacher examine Talya, walks over and holds Talya's hand. They stand together and follow the retreating figures with their eyes. Then they take a turn on the swings. Talya kicks her feet high and soars through the air, smiling at the sensation of weightlessness.

Cyclone

WE WERE WALKING IN the middle of the snow-covered street, up the steep hill from the café, steadying each other on the ice. Candy was a puffy, gray blob in her down jacket with the hood up. So was I, I suppose, in mine.

"Lonny," Candy said, after we'd been walking a while, "when you leave me, I want to know. Promise you won't just disappear."

"I'm not going to leave you."

"I'm easy to leave, I always have been. Just remember what I said, all right?"

"I'm not going to leave you."

I looked at her, but she chose not to look back. I put my hand on her coat collar and massaged her neck — at least made the motions of doing it through the down. I didn't say any more; better not to step on her little moments of melodrama, but they made me crazy.

In the beginning, I never admitted I loved her. When she pressed me, as she often did then, way too soon I thought, I sang her the first line of a song that said bluntly: The minute you let yourself care, there will not be anyone there. The song's statement struck me as adequate explanation of my reluctance. Unfortunately, after she heard the album often enough that it was familiar, she began coming back at me with the next line, to the affect that this time it's different. In that, as in all her determined little ways, she refused to let me stay at a safe distance. When do you admit you love a person? Somewhere along the line, I couldn't bear the thought of her not being there. Only she never quite seemed to believe it.

For her, the signs were everywhere and they were all black and white. "We made love once last week. Do you realize that?" was how she confronted me in the shower when I was already late for work.

And now, with her so wary, so volatile, I was reminding myself again of that line from the song. I particularly did not like hearing the name Charles so often. Mister all-knowing, too-friendly, too-helpful from her law school class. "Don't be silly," she had passed that off. We were — this at least I could see clearly — in the paranoid phase of our relationship.

"Twice," I replied to her, as we switched places so I could rinse off the soap. Bubbles sprayed her shoulder and sailed away down her breast. She shivered until I let her back under the water. She was one skinny length of goose bumps, weighed down with a soggy mat of brown where her curls usually were. Still pretty, soaking wet. Prettier even, in her vulnerability. And she still did turn me on, despite her conviction that I found her just less enticing than a broccoli stalk.

"Lonny, it doesn't count as twice if we do it at night and then again the next morning. That's one incidence of passion. One continuous incident."

I rolled my eyes. "Is this like the single-transaction test in civil procedure? You're not a lawyer yet, you know. Talk like a human being for a little while longer."

The slap from her wet wash cloth echoed in the steamy whiteness of the shower and for a moment she was afraid she had hurt me. "Anyway," she said when she found that she had not, "twice isn't much better than once."

So here we were tonight, on the ice, slipping along, returning from the café. We had been sitting at the bar, the panorama of Manhattan before us and the spires and spokes of the bridge above.

A man in a captain's hat pushed up next to Candy's chair to give his order in a painfully hoarse voice. He was leaning over the bar with the eyes of a bird of prey, ready to pounce on every move the bartender made, commenting on every ingredient that swirled into his drink. He continued to rasp across us, an annoying buzz that wouldn't stop. Candy asked me what a cyclone was. "You" was what came immediately to mind, but I subdued the thought, and told her that I hadn't the faintest idea.

I whispered to Candy that she ought not accuse *me* of being fussy and anal after seeing this guy. I knew she would not resist temptation for long. She asked him finally what the drink was that was being so painstakingly concocted for him. She asked it in that self-effacing tone pretty little girls learn early in life to use with certain men. I cringed. She sensed it or saw it in the bar mirror and her eyes flashed with anger. Her tone, of course, was successful and brought us a hoarse lecture on sidecars, not cyclones; she had heard it wrong.

With his arms moving, his fingers pressing too often against Candy's shoulder and forearm, he went on and on about the inability of bartenders to make real sidecars. He had come upon sidecars in some thirties novel I never heard of, and made it his own. "It's a class drink," he told us. "Today, the way things are — look at this turkey." He shook his head in the direction of the bartender. "Triple Sec instead of Cointreau, really?" He insisted we taste the finished product. Additionally flawed, he said, because this bar used liquid sweetener instead of bar sugar. "They all do," he told us, shaking his head.

Candy engaged him in conversation well beyond a reasonably polite period. She saw that I was annoyed. "He was an interesting character" was all she offered when he was gone. We drank in silence.

"Isn't it pretty as a picture?" she said, breaking the silence. I looked out at the night. The span of the bridge arched in dots of light. Behind it the skyscrapers of Manhattan glowed. It was a post card picture from here, where you couldn't see what was going on behind all those lights.

"What does your friend Charles think of the prospect of exams?" I asked with what I hoped was a biting formality.

She glanced over at me and shrugged. "Don't know," she said. "I haven't talked to him."

Now we were walking back to her place in Brooklyn Heights. The streets were silent, carless, frosty. The apartment was warm. She put her diaphragm in before we went to bed, but we just went to sleep.

In the morning, I lay under the covers warm with her, except where the cold of the winter Saturday brushed my exposed face. I put my head under the covers and lay against her heat, wrapped in her smell, gazing out through the blanket weave at the bright sunny day and the brittle, brown remains of a spider plant hanging in the window. Its demise was not a surprise; it amused me though that she had left it for so many months, apparently liking its particular deadness.

I examined her home, her crowded, untidy collection of stuffed animals and books and crystal vases and posters of ballet dancers. To the world, I suppose I should say, she was Candice, and always had been. She even acted like a Candice out there — mature, sophisticated, demure. I alone, with the exception of her incorrigible father, was permitted to call her Candy, but only in private. The impulse had been irresistible in the super-passionate beginning, you know, sweet, creamy, all that. I must say, given all that, I had a moment's pause each time her father called her Candy. I kidded her once about it and she smacked me in the face. "Anyway, he's not my father; step-father," she said. That gave me a further moment's pause. Hmm, so if something was going on, it would be OK?

"Well, he's sure been giving a good imitation for twenty-five years," I said. Her "real" father had quit the scene early. She had sought him out her first year in law school.

Candy's cat dove off the dresser onto my pillow and stuck his wet nose in Candy's cheek. She had called him Elephant when he was a kitten, but, overfed and fawned over, he grew so humongous that we changed his name to Petunia. Candy picked herself up on one arm and stroked his head. "Hi, Tunee, little Tunee." She lay back down and stretched, reached out and lifted him and held him suspended in air. He looked like a cat balloon, legs outstretched, paw pads spread, little whiskers all pointing down.

She hugged him, and he scampered away. Then it was my turn. "My little fambily," she sing-songed as she hugged me. A hug led to a kiss and a kiss to a frenzy of lovemaking. The suddenness of the shift left the cat perplexed. I caught a glimpse of him sitting on the stereo, blinking down at us.

"Should I have put in more cream?" Candy asked afterwards.

The pillow sank as Petunia landed.

"What a good, discrete kitty," Candy said, gathering up the cat and rocking him back and forth. He began struggling, wriggled free, and sat in the doorway, preening himself. "Go ahead, repair all the damage, wash every hair I touched, get 'em all." Candy banged her fist up and down on my hip. "Should-I-have-put-in-more-cream?" I didn't have an answer.

Candy lay back down, wriggling into the pillow. "You know, I was a mistake," she said.

"You're telling me," I agreed enthusiastically. That, I realized even before her face wrinkled up, was a mistake on my part.

She stood and disappeared into the bathroom. I scratched Petunia's ear, wondering if I should call in to her that I was sorry. From the bed I could see myself in her full-length mirror. It had stood against a wall for months. Then one day I walked in to find her beaming proudly at me and at the mirror hanging on the bathroom door; it was disconcerting to see myself headless. She had hung it at her height.

When she walked out, she started to comb her hair. She ignored my presence. Then she turned and said, "I hate it when you leave the toilet seat up, which you did again."

I might have responded with the tiniest twitch of a smile. I could not help finding humor in imagining her stumbling into the dark bathroom in the middle of the night and sitting down on nothing, sinking in. I quickly fought off the image, but she missed nothing.

She threw her hair brush on the dresser hard. Petunia jumped away from me. Then the clatter of the telephone pierced us both.

"Hello," she barked. I heard her struggle to present a cheerful voice. "Nothing," she said.

I wondered if it was her good friend Charles. Then I took a deep breath and sighed. I took in the sight of her. She stood in the sun rays that fanned through the dirty translucence of the windows. She looked so — so vulnerable, her little breasts barely jutting out from her ribs, her clinging blue panties accentuating her thin legs and small, firm rear end. The room was warm now, the steam scent of the radiator giving the room a somnolent coziness. Petunia passed back and forth against my legs. I walked up behind Candy as she talked, and rested my mouth against her neck, absorbing her heat.

"It was my father," she said as she hung up. She ran her hands down my sides.

"Which one?" I asked.

"The first one, the original, the one who made the mistake."

I pulled her middle close. She was elsewhere. Speaking with any of her three parents turned her morbid. She held back as I pulled her closer. She looked at me questioningly. "Do we love each other?" she asked, peering intently into my eyes. Hers wide, gray blue, searching my face.

"We love each other."

"Really? Do we really, really?"

"Really, really."

"But are you sure."

"I'm sure."

"Well that's good," she sing-songed.

"I *was* a mistake, you know."

"Not for me, you weren't."

She smiled. "That's nice of you to say."

We lay on the bed then, and she cradled me in her arms, stroking my hair. "They had already decided to get a divorce," she explained. "How could he just leave and never even come back to see his beautiful little girl?" She squinted down at me and whispered, "That's me, you know." Then she said, "He claims the court ordered it. I don't hardly buy that. Well, now he has his little child wife and his baby. I can't believe I have a baby sister."

"But," I said, "he's been very nice to you since you looked him up. You said yourself you used to go there weekends before we met, your first year in law school, when it was so tough, and they used to feed you and treat you like a queen."

"Guilt."

"Maybe not."

"A free baby sitter, that's all."

I cocked my head at her.

"Baby sitters are hard to find. Who cares? Who needs him. Or her. Or my bitch mother, for that matter."

Her mother was indeed something of a bitch. "You have me."

"Or her husband, who doesn't even have enough respect for me to call me by my right name."

"You have me."

"I have you," she said mechanically.

I frowned, feeling hurt. Why did my mind flash a glimpse of Charles.

"I have my cat!" Candy said enthusiastically, and jumped up, and swooped Petunia into her arms. He scrambled free and dove under the bed. "Even my cat doesn't want me." She made a pouting face.

"I want you." I suppose that declaration was not exactly drenched in emotion. I was tired of this conversation.

"Sometimes you want me. Sometimes you do," she said, laying her cheek against my chest. "You're a good boy, Lonny."

—◆—

Now it was midyear exam time. Candy and her friend Judy were awash in paper at the dining room table in my apartment. It was twilight and they had not yet turned on the lamp. I watched from the kitchen, crying over the onion I was chopping, having agreed out of sheer benevolence to feed them while they studied.

"Lonny, honey, more coffee."

"Christ, Cand, you're gonna float away, if you don't blast off."

"Lonny, more coffee, less noise," Candy said.

Judy raised her eyebrows at me playfully and I shrugged. I made decaffeinated and brought it over, turning on the light by the table and closing the curtains.

"Thanks, Hon," Candy said.

"Umm, good coffee," Judy said. "Did you ever think of renting yourself — 'houseman to the working woman?'" The way she eyed me sometimes, I had the feeling she'd like to be my first rental customer.

The coffee didn't fool Candy. She slapped the table. "Damn it, stop trying to run my life. Why can't you just make coffee and not decide for me whether I should have regular or decaf?"

Judy looked confused as she put down her cup.

"We'll be eating soon," I said to Candy.

She gave me a dirty look and then ignored me. Arthur, my cat, was kicking around one of the crumpled yellow sheets of paper they had discarded. I left him that one, but picked up the others. As I stooped, I caught Judy's eyes on me again. A year ago, if I had met her, I would have tried to steal her. I never cheated on anyone, but I didn't really, I suppose, have scruples in the other direction. I could feel the sparks, but it was not an issue. I did love Candy. I smiled.

When I was back in the kitchen and Judy was looking the other way, Candy mouthed a kiss at me, and smiled a thank you for putting up with her little exam-week outbursts.

The vegetables sizzled, the rice cooked, and then I made Candy clear the table so I could set it properly and we could all eat a civilized meal. "He's such a damned perfectionist," Candy complained, "always wanting to make life like a painting or something."

"Hard to paint a perfect cyclone," I said.

"Don't knock the service," Judy replied to Candy's comment. "My boyfriend calls me in the morning before each exam to wish me luck; other than that, he's gone for the duration."

"The service is fine, but I'll never be perfect enough for him."

"Oh bull," I said. I stuck my tongue out at her. "She has a zit on her right tit," I told Judy. "Flawed."

Candy said, reflecting, "The zit's bigger than my tit."

Later on, I left them to their all-nighter with the tax code, and went to bed. Under the pillow I found a note, with a heart and a smiling little stick figure of a girl with lots of curls. "Thanks for taking care of me," the little girl said. She used to leave me notes in unexpected places all the time in the beginning.

At four-seventeen, according to my alarm clock's digital numbers, Judy's giggling awakened me. They were punch drunk and gossiping about the people in their class. All at once I realized Candy was talking about Charles and I came fully awake. She had gradually stopped mentioning his name a number of weeks ago. But apparently only to me had she stopped talking about him.

I listened intently, but Candy had fallen silent suddenly as if she had paused to take a drink. I waited to hear more, but Judy asked her a question about section something of some code. I cursed to myself.

The bedroom was shadowy, the clock's read-out casting a blue light. The chill of the winter night air went through me and I was glad when Arthur padded over and settled down against my arm; the sound of him licking his tail was loud. They were now in a big discussion of a tax code issue.

When I awoke in the morning, they were gone. That afternoon, she took the exam. I left work early, so I could surprise her. I watched the final minutes through the window in the classroom door: my pretty, soon-to-be-born lawyer with the bags under her eyes raising edifices from words like depreciation and basis and capital loss carryover. She had a sickly smile stuck on her face as she dropped her pen and slumped down. I backed away from the door and waited at a distance. She dropped her books at her locker and shared expressions of despair with her fellow students. Not with Charles. I watched him leave the room, glance at her walking away down the hall and turn in the other direction.

She smiled when I came up behind and tapped her on the shoulder. She rested her exhausted head against mine and sighed. "Oh Lonny, thank God it's over. Do you think I did OK?" she asked.

"No one does OK. They make it impossibly hard and if you show a glimmer of comprehension, you get an A. But you always feel as if you're screwing up." She thought about that, and then her eyes darted into direct contact with mine, as if to see if my words were meant to be summing us up.

We walked on the Promenade. It was too cold out, but the wrinkled old people lined the benches. The mothers pushed baby carriages. Young couples like us strolled, hand in hand. This was the place people came to be clichés for a few minutes out of their busy schedules. The crisp sea smell was tangy. The boats loomed like giant arks in their berths, and the giantess Liberty held her torch into the sun.

Candy was talking about a legal case from the exam. I remembered that case from law school. I told her why I thought the dissent was right. Her face fell. Whoops. I reassured her the argument could be made either way. It was how well you made it that mattered. Her warm rear end pressed against my hand that rested in the back pocket of her jeans as we walked. We fell silent for many steps.

"Lonny," she said, all of a sudden turning to me with a tense, drawn look on her face, "there's something I have to tell you."

I knew what was coming was made possible by a night without sleep. I felt myself going limp, sure of what she was about to say.

"There's something," she said again. "Now that exams are over with and I can think. It's old news, all right? Not current. Just something that happened. It doesn't matter. It's really been on my mind though. It's eating at me. I don't want you to find out some other way, Judy or someone."

A chill twisted through me as I stared at her. I felt nauseous.

Her face, close to mine, was dry with winter, and pale. Her lips were cracked. Below her pale eyes, through which I was peering into her, were dark, deep circles. Her fingers played in my hair, insistently.

I had assured her once that there could be no way back from such a transgression. The end. My mind spun.

"I love you, Lonny. Please believe me."

I was walking away from her and she was running to keep up. I kept walking and she kept running.

In Saint-Rémy And Auvers

S UNLESS DAY OUT STEVEN's window. Me talking to Steven from the bathroom. Oh. Wave of queasy feeling. Slump down on the toilet; the cold stings my bottom.

Have to finish putting on my makeup. Steven pacing. Knows I'll be late as usual. I won't this time. He's been waiting for today. I'm trying to push myself — for him. I don't care about it that much. Surface. Color chart games. "That whole century was pretty, but what beyond light?" I say.

Steven comes in. His face in the mirror gets me so hot. I bend forward toward the sink. He presses close. Forget the whole show, he's starting to think, I know he wants to now, just drag me to bed; but he also really wants to see Van Gogh. And it's the last chance.

"The old Dutch," I continue what I was saying. "The whole world, everything — sadness, suffering, understanding, good- ness — is painted into the expression of a Rembrandt face. Everything. The man was a genius. It's as simple as that." I dab eyeliner on crooked, hurrying too much. Have to wipe it off.

Annoys him, that expression. Simple as that. Nothing is "as simple as that," his usual response. I try the eyeliner again; see my face contorted in the mirror: mouth stretched open, cheek pulled flat, eye yanked wide. Him watching. Wondering if we'll be late; more than that, wanting a decision, wanting to know our future. Just to know, whichever it is going to be. I waver. How can I make up my mind? How can I?

He is looking at me. "I'm almost ready," I say. My panties and bra betray me. And one eye yet unpainted. Everything is such an effort. "I'm almost ready," I repeat.

I view this body in the mirror. Touch my stomach lightly. "I really think I'm bigger; why don't you see it?"

He turns away, smiling. "You're being absurd," he says to the door.

The marble lobby of faces, the colliding babble, it's overwhelming. I cling to Steven's hand. Pulling me along. Weaving me through the crowd. I don't feel agile. Get tangled up with a palsied woman. Try to duck around her, still holding fast to Steven. She is ruffled — shaking, twitching. "Excuse me," I whisper, looking away. Concentrate on holding tight the things my free hand wraps: my jacket, my tote bag, purse, my book. Steven says why don't I put the book in the tote bag. "Oh," I say. "I didn't think of it." It feels like too much effort. Easier to just hold it. Also the paper bag from the deli with the biscuits. Steven insisted we stop. He's had this idea something like them would help me. I didn't think so. Stopping almost made us late. But they seemed to help.

Steven handing in our tickets. Walking toward the headphones. I don't want any. "Philippe the Mellow Bellow," he urges. I shake my head. He smiles. He's happy. It makes me happy. Crowd murmuring and babbling; we walk in.

Suddenly paintings. Long walls of heavy frames. Silence. Hush. The guard's soles squeaking.

"How are you feeling?"

"OK, I guess."

"Don't you want me to carry something?" he asks as he has twice before.

"No, I'm OK."

Steven bends and kisses my cheek. I edge up to him. My ear. My neck. I let go his hand and reach around his neck, pull him down to me, kiss him hard. "I love you," I say into his mouth. He says he loves me. He presses my head to his chest, caresses me. I feel safe again at first. Like I can make this decision. It's really two decisions. Marriage. We have not ever spoken that little word.

He sees my look. Says, "Let's not talk about it. Let's let it go for now. The right answer will appear. The moment will come when you know."

"We don't have much more time." Tears are rushing out of my eyes. It's all so easy and rational in his mind. You lay out the pluses and minuses, as we have. Then you decide. And you don't look back. He lives on the surface. He doesn't understand.

I can't think about it anymore. Peer around. Stop in front of a painting. This mass of color dazzling me before I focus, before I see. It glows. I start to focus on it. A field of wheat. Luxuriant. Fecund. Ripening wheat; blackberries; stately green cypress; violet hills; pale blue sky. It takes my breath.

Next, olive orchards. Canvas after canvas. Violets and greens. Blues and reds. Swirls and jags. Yellows ablaze. I am startled to like all this so much, glad Steven forced me to get dressed and out.

I see him across the room. Walk there. Stand in front of a self-portrait of the artist, green-tinted and unearthly, ascending from a violet darkness. Steven is staring at it. Somehow knows it's me come up. Feels me. "He was my age. I'm as old as he was," he says. I touch his back.

He was so young, I think. There could have been so much more, I think. I know that isn't what Steven meant — he's feeling sorry for himself. He's despairing: look at all this man did and his own life is a failure. I've done nothing, he is thinking. I've created nothing.

Steven turns from the picture. His hazel eyes I love. But I was wrong. There is hope in them — I see now what he meant: even if nothing is right in his life, he is still alive. He will live to be older than the famous artist.

Yellow sun. Washes an entire sky. Burnishes olive orchards to hot orange. Steven leads me on, through fields of poppies, trees, orchards.

"Steven. He killed himself." This fact suddenly new. Frightening. Don't want to believe it. Ended all this with a gunshot. I find myself walking slower. Steven pulling me along, keeping me moving. I want to hold it back — this act already decided.

"I don't feel so good, honey." Clutching the jacket. Feeling the paper bag slip. Have barely the energy to tighten my grip on it.

Steven pries the jacket from me.

"Give me the book now." My fingers unclench. "Now the bag."

I feel emptied. Weightless. He takes my hand. I am bent forward. Leads me to a wooden bench in the center of the room. A woman all folds of fat heaves herself to the side, making room. I must look awful. I hate to cause a stir.

"Thank you," I whisper. She is already looking away, not to intrude.

Steven moves me like clay, pushes me down, pressing my shoulders. I am so small next to this woman. Steven kneels in front of me, stroking my hair. His eyes look like they are going to well over.

"I'm OK," I say.

"Are you going to throw up?" he asks, caressing me.

"I don't think so," I say after considering.

He is fumbling in the bag, pulling out the box of biscuits. He hands me a biscuit — places it in my palm, closes my fingers on it, lifts my hand to my mouth. I bite. The crumbs sprinkle on my sweater, my jeans. I chew mechanically, staring blankly at the crumbs on the peach thread; grind the cracker to paste. Make the effort to swallow.

"I love these," I say. Two paintings in front of us, side by side. I feel as if I'm with Vincent, standing outside this rain-streaked wheat field, all plum blues and violets, soggy, through this un-crossable screen of droplets.

The biscuit isn't helping. I bend down, lower my head slowly between my legs, trying to press my palms through the dizziness in my forehead. "Oh God I feel sick."

Steven is rubbing my neck. I hear his voice in this blur.

I hear him saying words. Words of on the one hand, on the other.

I nod at whatever he just said.

"Here." Steven gives me a fresh biscuit from the package. Brushes crumbs off my sweater.

"I don't think they're helping anymore, honey."

"Should we just go?" Steven says.

"No," I say. I caress his wrist, say quietly, "Just let me sit for a minute." I feel this wave of heat roll over me. "It'll pass."

"Let me go see how much more there is," he says. "You sit here for a minute."

"I'm sorry."

"Don't be." He pats my head. Merges into the crowd.

I sit hunched over, gaze at the rain. And next to it the same field in the bright sun. A white round sun, radiating a great yellow halo across the entire sky, casting its streaks of light on the long vertical rows of grain reaching to the horizon. What did he think about right before he stuck the gun in his stomach? When he felt the pressure of the shaft against his middle and still had not pulled the trigger?

Steven says it is worth going on, all the double square canvases at the end are spectacular. But I can not seem to look at the pictures without thinking about Vincent's end.

We leave Saint-Rémy and enter Auvers. We hit a big crowd of people who are in a celebratory mood. They bother me. Laughter; chatter. Two men bump me talking about Chinese food they are dying for: Buddhist's delight, lemon chicken, sesame noodles.

Have trouble getting near the pictures here. Have to squeeze in. Jostled.

Steven has gotten way ahead of me. Now he is walking back, face pinched in concern. His hand feels warm. He leads me. Stops with me to examine paintings.

We pass through another doorway, another room. Painting after painting. We walk on.

"This is the last room now, isn't it?

"Uh huh."

I look in from the doorway. Vast canvases. Long. The double squares. I can survey them all from here. Something strikes me and I scan the room again. It's the sun. "Do you notice something?" I say. "Look back," I say. "I'm pretty sure," I say, turning him around, leading him back away from the last room. To where Auvers begins. "Do you see it now?" I say. "What's missing." Steven is perplexed. "There isn't a sun," I say. "There's no sun in Auvers. Anywhere. Not in one picture." Steven looks around him, surprised. And we walk back to be sure. There is no sun.

I face these pictures, wishing I could tell Vincent not to do it.

A wheat field, an unbearable horizontal vastness. As if Vincent looked into time itself and saw this clouded dark plane of blue settling over these cold whitened greens. Neither plane with a drop of solace.

To my left, the crows. I inch toward it. I stare into its chaos, so familiar. The jagged strokes of pigment at war. Black blue sky wrenching itself away from angry yellow wheat. Green paths that can't be followed. That go nowhere. I realize suddenly that everything is all wrong. These paths are all joining at the bottom instead of at the horizon they never reach, the reverse perspective pushing the picture down on me. And the horrible crows descend. Their leader emerging from a swirl of translucent green cloud, like some awful hatching devil. I want Vincent to have turned these paths around. I look for a next canvas, but this is all there is.

In the marble lobby, Steven holds my hand and asks me do I want to go see the Rembrandts while we're here. It's sweet of him. But no.

Through the wintry park we walk, homeward, holding hands. Talking of painting, of complementary colors and opposite colors. He is revived, resolved to start anew on his own work, dreaming aloud. He has his arm around my neck and turns to kiss me as we walk. "I love you," he says, hot. We are hurrying home now; my mouth is dry, my armpits damp. This hasn't changed since day one. High stepping up the stairs, we bang the door open, fling off our jackets, roll into bed. My foot is kicking his underpants over his ankle and off. We get hotter and hotter having nothing between us, and saying words about what's in me, what we did.

Then we are lying together in the stillness. Steven falls asleep. I stare without seeing. Steven is rational. He just asks me to weigh and decide. Me. All I see are Vincent's paths, incongruously converging, each one a wrong choice. Bearing down on me.

To Grandmother's House We Go

VICTORIA MORRIS AND HER young son Lanny stepped from the airliner into dazzling white sunlight and steaming tropical heat. The towering palms gave her a momentary good feeling, a fleeting sense of being someplace different, exotic, out of herself, before the assaulting brightness brought tears to her eyes. Victoria squinted as she pulled Lanny across the shimmering asphalt toward the relief of air-conditioned dimness. Once inside the terminal building, she stood for a moment, closing her eyes until the glow behind her lids faded. The tingle of cool perspiration on her bare arms brought instant relief.

It had just been winter, a kind of cozy gray indifference blanketing her. "Victoria, dear, it's Mom calling. If you want to see your grandmother alive you had better come now" was the message she had found on her answering machine. She picked up the phone to call her grandfather.

"Well, it don't look good, what can I tell you. We doin' the best that we can, but it don't look good. She won't eat. What can you do?"

"But is Mommy exaggerating as usual or is it — "

"Well, it's a matter of time. How much time who knows. You should come down. If you can manage it. I don't know how much longer I got either, you know what I mean? I'm ninety-one next month. I'd like to see you. It's been a long time." That plaintive voice. "Maybe I can help you out a little with the plane. I got room you can stay."

"No," she said, "It'd be more comfortable at Walter's." Knowing her grandfather's offer was certain to come, she had her answer ready. She would confirm with her brother later. If he said no, she would get a hotel room. It gave her the creeps just thinking of staying in that filthy apartment.

"I got room," her grandfather repeated, and then was silent, leaving her with a familiar pinching feeling in her chest. "Whatever you wanna do," he said after a pause.

❖

When she blinked her eyes open in the terminal, Victoria saw her mother, Sylvia Morris, poised, a study in posed anticipation. She was carefully decked out in gray pants — probably a size two, they still bagged on her — and a red blouse with a bow in front. Her face looked old, wrinkled beyond her years. Her dark eyes stared intently into the flow of arriving travelers. Victoria walked toward her, clutching Lanny by the hand.

It became increasingly apparent to Victoria as she approached ever closer that her mother, who was now nervously twitching a cigarette up and down in the corner of her red, puckered mouth, did not recognize her. This was disconcerting. Her mother was straining against the felt rope, frowning now into the crowd. Still looking elsewhere for the perfect daughter, Victoria thought.

"Hi, Mom."

"Oh my God!" her mother said, in a booming hoarse voice, peering dramatically up at Victoria and down at Lanny and back up at Victoria. "Victoria, I didn't recognize you. Do you believe it? Oh my God. Can you believe that?" She threw herself around Victoria, hugging her. Then she stood with her hands on her hips, shaking her head. "This is Lanny?" she asked. "Victoria. Oh, Victoria."

"What's wrong?" Lanny asked his mother.

"Nothing's wrong," Sylvia boomed an answer. "What do you think? You're gorgeous. You're such a little man. I haven't seen you in five long years. You were just this high." Her hand vibrated as she held it out from her body.

"I know," Lanny said, reasonably.

Victoria felt the accusation knotting in her stomach. "Three years, Mom."

"Three, five. A long time. Victoria, let me look at you. Have you lost weight? My God, I can't believe I didn't recognize you! You look so good. What did you do with your hair? It looks great."

Translation: Last time I saw you — many years ago — you were rather pudgy, you didn't look your best, your hair just hung there.

"Thanks, Mom," Victoria said.

"You look so good."

"Thanks, Ma."

"I'm making you the *best* dinner. Veal scallopini, and I baked your favorite, a cherry pie. I've been cooking since early this morning. We'll eat at Grampa's. There's no room to move at my place, and I don't want to start imposing on Walter and Rhonda."

"You shouldn't have, Ma."

"What, my only daughter comes to visit after four years, what do you think, we're not going to celebrate?"

The baggage collected, they stepped through the sliding doors into the neat rows of lush vegetation, into the ambushing light, into the heat that baked bright colors into pastels.

Victoria fumbled for her inaccessible sunglasses, her bags threatening to tumble her over. Lanny started whining that he had a headache, was hungry, wanted to swim.

The car was so mercifully cool. Out the window, the palms and flowers gave way fast to flat wasteland, scrub trees and tall grasses extending to a horizon dotted with clusters of bleak residential development.

"How much longer?" Lanny said.

"Not long dear," Sylvia's raspy voice answered.

------◄O►------

On the catwalk outside Grampa's condominium, everyone was helping bring things up from Sylvia's car. "Watch that pie," Sylvia's stentorian voice cut through the thick, hot air. She was standing by her car, hands on out-thrust hips, neck craning up, eyes two fiery suns of tinted glass aimed at them. Lanny stopped in his tracks from a lope, then stepped gingerly toward the door where pots and aluminum-foil-covered plates sat on the catwalk. Victoria's brother, Walter, came along behind with more pots of food, and stooped to pick up the pie.

"Be careful with that pie. I'll kill you."

Victoria was in the small kitchen unwrapping and trying to make room, trying not to see how filthy everything was. Walter stuck his head out the door, and shouted down at his mother, "Watch the pie, Ma." Lanny had found the television in the den and was watching a movie he knew he wasn't supposed to watch.

"Don't tell Mom," he pleaded with Walter. "Just say it's some movie."

"No problem. It's our secret," his Uncle Walter said, as Victoria approached, looking for Lanny. "He's in there, watching some movie. It's OK, it's a perfectly OK movie."

"Lanny, turn it off now."

Grampa was hovering, surveying the goings on. "You want a soda? Come on, have a soda. Sure."

"Is it cold?"

"There's ice in the freezer, what are you talking about?"

"No, that's OK." She wouldn't use anything from his refrigerator.

"Vic," Walter said where only she could hear, "it's all right. I brought a bag of ice."

Victoria didn't ask why Rhonda and the kids weren't coming.

Sylvia was handing dishes through the pass-through from the kitchen to the dining end of the living room. Victoria was placing them on the already-crowded table.

"Sit down everyone," Sylvia called out. "Lanny, sit down at the table, dear. Here, Victoria, take this plate of veal."

"Walter," Grampa said, appearing out of the kitchen carrying a slab of red meat on its wrapping paper, "how about a nice steak? A beautiful piece of meat, it will go to waste. I bought it yesterday. Twelve dollars it cost. Come on. I can cook it right up for you."

"No, that's OK, Grampa. Mommy's prepared a ton of food. We won't go hungry."

"Of course, of course, but it's a shame to waste."

Sylvia came around the kitchen door carrying a large tureen of noodles. "What's he doing? I don't believe him."

"A nice piece of steak. I'm just asking. What's so terrible?"

"Are you crazy? I spent the whole day preparing this meal. What's the matter with you? Put that away. Walter, sit down. He — is— going — to — drive — me — completely — out — of — my — mind! What's wrong with you?"

"I'm just asking."

"Well don't ask."

———— ◄O► ————

Victoria felt as if the meal would go on all night. She asked Walter if he would mind taking her over to the hospital before it got too late.

"Why don't you wait until tomorrow?" her grandfather said. "You had a long day, after all. You have some dessert, then get settled at Walter's."

"Yeah," Sylvia said, "what's the hurry?"

"Vicky," Walter said, "Ma, be quiet; she wants to go. You want to go, I'll take you."

"A'right, so we'll all go," Grampa said. "You want to go tonight, so we'll go. I donno what for."

Victoria was annoyed that they were all coming to the hospital. They packed into the car as if they were going to a fast-food place. Walter drove, Sylvia sat in the front. She, Lanny, and Grampa were wedged in the back.

When they reached the hospital, Victoria walked toward her grandmother's room with trepidation, holding Lanny tightly by the hand. Lanny was unusually quiet. His eyes darted into all the rooms they passed, with their half-dressed figures on the beds, withered bodies expelling assorted moans and a chorus of "Nurse!" His face was rigid, devoid of its usual expressiveness, and his step stiff. She had tried to seem cheerful, but she knew he sensed her anxiety.

"This is it," Sylvia whispered loudly.

Victoria stopped walking, and looked into the bare room, at the empty first bed with the length of drab curtain hanging down and pushed back in the corner. Everything in her was resisting looking the other way.

Slowly she turned, feeling now the drag of Lanny holding back. She had tried to steel herself against this moment. But tears started forming in her eyes as she saw her grandmother, spotted first the tubes taped to her nose. She felt in her tingling skin the violation it must be, and the discomfort. Her grandmother seemed to be asleep, a pudgy, pale face and a shock of feather-thin, white hair in a mountain of blanket and sheet and pillow and gown and her own corpulence. Her eyes flickered open, unseeing.

"Hi, Grandma," Victoria said softly. Lanny was pressing up against Victoria and she put her arm around him.

Her grandmother's eyes squinted without her eyeglasses, and stared for a moment, not really seeing anything, and then closed.

"It's Vicky, Grandma."

Her eyes opened again. Victoria had been dreading this unknowing stare. In anticipation, this non-recognition had been, to her, annihilating. She thought that, with the exception of Lanny, her grandmother was probably the only person alive who took genuine pleasure from her existence on the earth. And in ways she tried to convince herself were absurd, the withdrawal of that acknowledgement of her being was opening a blackness in her that she feared.

"Veekee." Her grandmother's voice was just audible.

"My God, can you believe this?" Victoria heard her mother bellow. Sylvia, Walter, and Grampa were standing just inside the door. "She has been a vegetable for weeks. She didn't even know who I was."

"Ma," Walter said. "She can hear you."

"Ah," Sylvia grunted, waving her arm.

"It's Vicky, Grandma."

Her grandmother started to raise her hand to the tubes in her nose, but her hand stopped short, and Victoria suddenly became aware of the bindings around her wrists. "She's tied down!" she said, turning sharply to her mother and grandfather behind her.

Her grandfather answered with that tone of resignation in his voice that she was coming to despise, "Yes, well, what can you do, the doctor — " and her mother interrupted in an agitated voice, "She keeps ripping the tubes out of her nose. She won't listen."

Victoria felt sick in her stomach. She took her grandmother's hand, lowered it to the bed, and stroked her arm lightly. "How are you feeling?"

"Oh, Veekee," she said, again trying to raise her right hand, which was anchored securely to the railing of the bed.

"Are you feeling OK?" Victoria found herself shouting for her to hear.

"OK."

"Can I do anything for you?"

"What?"

Victoria looked over her shoulder and asked her grandfather, sitting now in a chair and staring off into space, "Where is her hearing aid?"

"Back at the place, you know. They didn't bring it. We'll get it. Don't worry."

"Can I get you anything, Grandma?"

"How is the baby?"

"I brought Lanny," Victoria said, "the baby."

"I'm not a baby," Lanny broke in, insulted. He had been standing quietly, seriously, leaning forward.

"Lanny, the baby."

"Veekee — I'm so heppy to see you."

Victoria was bending over to hear the frail whisper, but she was elated because her grandmother was talking, and they told her she wouldn't talk, and she recognized her, and in her broken trembling whisper, she kept talking, clinging to Victoria's hand, not wanting to let her go. Victoria didn't understand all she said, in part, she thought because her grandmother's false teeth were not in her mouth. Apparently they too had been left at the home, and no one had gone to get them.

"How's the baby?"

"He's right here," Victoria said, pushing him in front of her.

"Hi Grandma," Lanny said, his face rigid, his voice tremulous.

"This is Lanny."

"Lanny?"

"The baby."

"How is the baby?"

"She don't understand," her grandfather said. "Dis is the baby, Victoria's baby, he's not a baby anymore."

"Veekee," she said again, "Veekee."

"I love you, Grandma."

Victoria's grandfather was rising out of the seat and walking up behind Victoria. "You better let her rest. Come on."

"Veekee."

"I'll see you tomorrow, Grandma," Victoria said, kissing her and standing up, still holding her clinging hand. Her grandfather edged up to the bed and leaned over as Victoria stepped away. All at once, Victoria realized that he was going to kiss his wife. Victoria couldn't remember when she had seen him do that. He was prying her hand from Victoria's.

"Goodbye dear," he said, groping awkwardly for the clamped hand. As he bent low to kiss her cheek, Victoria's grandmother abruptly turned her face away.

Victoria knew, glancing at her mother, that like a carnivore with a carcass, Sylvia would not let go her hold on this morsel. She would chew it, swallow it, savor it.

"She's tired," her grandfather said, his face draining of color. He straightened up and stepped back, "Come on, let's go. We'll have dinner."

"Dinner," Sylvia said, "What, are you crazy? We just ate a huge dinner."

"Oh, right, I don't know what I'm thinking. You'll come back to my apartment. We'll have dessert."

"Watch the cherry pie, Lanny," Walter said.

"It's going to be great. You'll love it," Sylvia said.

Boiling Water

"My name is Michael Aaron," Michael said into the telephone, the sound of the words in the air stiff, hollow, and strange after hearing them, reciting them in his head for so long. He hurried on before Annie could interrupt him, or, worse yet, hang up. "I met you some time ago," he said. "I know it's a long while, but I hoped you may remember me. I just thought I'd give it a try, give you a call. I hope you don't mind."

She was still listening, so he hurtled on. "If you're free, I'd very much like to take you to dinner." He was hesitating then, but didn't want to give her a chance to speak yet. "I know a nice restaurant on Columbus Avenue, Warin's, maybe you've been there?" Now he waited. He could hear her breathing and the clicking static of the telephone connection. No words came from her though, and he was trying to think what he should say next.

But finally she spoke. "Where did I meet you?" she asked tentatively, in a clipped, careful, but conversational tone. It was such a simple question to be such a weighty answer. Michael could not stop a smile from creasing his tension. Relief made the phone feel heavy on his ear. But he gave his answer in a flat, even voice, just as he had given it in his mind all week.

"Bonnie Williat, in your building," he said. "I was a friend of hers."

"Bonnie, yes," she said slowly, "I do remember you. Sure, it would be very nice to have dinner, maybe tomorrow."

About ten minutes past eight the next day, Michael stood in front of her apartment door, his palms moist all over again, his heart thumping. He heard the scrape of the latch, the clank of the locks, one after another. The door opened slowly, jerking, while behind it her voice, rising with irritation, scolded the cat. Then she appeared, a bent over side view and a distracted, "Come in quick, before he gets out. I don't want to chase him up the stairs."

Michael had pictured the moment differently.

Once the door was safely closed, however, she gave him her full attention. They stood a few feet apart in the entrance way. She seemed to lean forward with an energy barely held in check, almost as if she were standing on tip toes. This was more the picture he had envisioned.

She wore a summery, pale yellow skirt and a high-collared, high-shouldered, pleated blouse. He liked her in it. Her curly hair was long, as it had been two years before. She was petite, one might say, and shorter for being bare foot. He was taller. Her upturned face, her intent gray blue eyes were all encompassing, observing, wary now. He saw that she was nervous, but she was excited too.

They hovered momentarily, while the cat rubbed against their legs, meowing in the stillness. "Mickey," she began to speak, but he interrupted. "This is a nice apartment you have. Do you have it by yourself?

Annie looked at him for an instant, then answered, "Oh, yes, only me." Her body relaxed; it was as if she were coming off tiptoes. "How about you? Do you have your own place? Where do you live?"

He nodded and told her where. They stood awkwardly then.

"Your cat is very pretty," he said. The cat was kneading its paws on his ankle. He stooped to scratch its ear.

"He likes you," she said.

Michael smiled.

"I went with a guy a couple of years ago," Annie told him, eyes down-turned, "who Mr. Esmond really took to, just the way he's taking to you. Usually he doesn't take to people."

Their eyes met and they watched each other as Michael scratched the cat's neck. "I do like cats," he said. "So, shall we go?"

Walking down Columbus Avenue, Michael asked, "What kind of name is Mr. Esmond? I mean aside from being American alley cat."

In the movie, you know, Mr. Esmond learned to treat Lorelei Lee the way a girl should be treated. A woman, I mean."

"That's it there," Michael said, pointing.

"Yes," Annie said.

He held the door for her, and she thanked him.

"Let's sit in the garden," Annie said as the maître d' scooped two menus and started leading them to a table.

"Yes, it's nice in the garden," Michael said.

The restaurant was crowded. It had been loud inside. In the garden the babble was muffled and flat. "That table there," Annie said insistently to the maître d'.

"Whatever you like," he responded with tired tolerance, holding Annie's chair for her.

"This is nice," she said to Michael. The globed candles flickered on the tables. The breeze wafted warm, swaying the scattered evergreens and dwarf fruit trees.

"I was here once before," he said.

"Yes, I was too, once. I think I might have been sitting at this very table."

"Really? That's a coincidence."

"Yes, it's funny."

"Would you like something to drink?" Michael asked as the waiter, looking somewhat harried, appeared over them, nodding an acknowledgment to a waving hand some tables away.

"Yes please. I could use a drink."

They gave their orders and the waiter was gone.

Michael took a deep breath.

"So," Annie said.

"So," he said. What do you do?"

She smiled. "Didn't Bonnie tell you about me?"

"No, I don't see Bonnie anymore."

Annie gave him a look of surprise.

"I was involved with someone a while back who was also a friend of Bonnie's, and I discovered Bonnie was not, shall I say, a loyal friend."

"Really?" Annie said, toying with the edge of her menu. "That's surprising. I've always found her to be completely trustworthy."

"So what *do* you do?"

"Well, I passed the bar since I last saw you, and I work for a small law firm in midtown. I'm working real long hours, but it's pretty exciting. Heavy environmental caseload."

"That's good," he said. "I'm glad."

"You are?" she said, looking up at him. He nodded. "I'm glad you are," she said.

The drinks came. Michael thanked the waiter and picked up his glass. "Here's..." He thought for a moment.

She said, "Here's to *new* friends."

The waiter returned to take their dinner order. Michael said they needed more time, but Annie said, "No, that's OK; we know. You'll have the lasagna and for me eggplant Parmesan."

The waiter squinted at Michael, who gave a slight nod. The waiter wrote the order and was gone.

"So you were here before?" she asked then.

"Yes," he said. "I was here with an old girlfriend." He was fingering his fork, spinning it around on the paper mat, tracing the sketch of a vineyard in olive green shades. "It was our first date, actually."

"Really? That's a coincidence. I was here with an old boyfriend," Annie said. "About the same time. I wonder if we could have been sitting next to each other and not even known it. Tell me about her."

"Why?"

"Oh, break the ice, something to talk about. Do you mind? I mean if it's still difficult to talk about her..."

Michael replaced his fork and looked up at her. "Well, truthfully, it is usually."

Her mouth made a sad pout.

"But for some reason that I can't imagine, I sort of want to, if you don't mind."

"Not at all. Really. Did you, were you in love with her?"

"Well, you'll think I'm a syrupy – "

"Tell me," she said.

"I guess the truth is I loved her more than I've — it's like we were the same person, soulmates. Forgive me if that sounds trite."

"That close?" Her voice was barely audible. "So what happened?"

"Soulmates is perhaps not a good thing. We had an identity of needs and neuroses, perhaps. So when we hit each other's weakest points, it was like digging into our own sorest wounds and we responded to each other's weaknesses with — not with understanding or compassion."

"Sounds rather over-intellectualized to me. Perhaps you just couldn't get along. Perhaps you were just physically attracted and when you got beyond that, you had nothing in common."

"Do you really believe that?"

"I don't know. I don't know your ex-girlfriend. I was just thinking out loud. Was she pretty?"

"Yes, she was lovely. She was adorable. She looked a lot like you."

Michael smiled, but Annie said, "I hope you're not going out with me because I'm physically like her."

"She never thought I appreciated her looks, though."

"Maybe you never told her enough. Maybe she just needed to be reassured more that she was attractive."

"It may be."

"It sounds like you'd really like to be with her."

"Well, isn't that a little academic?"

"In a certain sense one could say that."

"I was probably just a physical thing for her. And, once that was over..."

"That is possible, but then," Annie said, lowering her eyes, "you know the guy I was here with. You know, that I told you before, I thought, when we broke up, it was pretty bad, it didn't end well, for months I must have gone out with every straight guy in the city."

"Wonderful."

"I just went out."

"Meaning?"

"I couldn't even get myself to kiss anyone. Really. They all repulsed me. Then I just wanted to be alone. I got to feel really strong being alone. I think before, I wanted guys to be my support."

"Like Lorelei wanted Mr. Esmond," he teased.

"Yeesss, be just like Mr. Esmond."

"And."

"Bonnie was a big help to me at that time," Annie continued. "Except she was always trying to fix me up with her friends."

"Bitch."

"Yes, I forgot you don't like her. My old boyfriend really got to dislike her also. I eventually started seeing someone."

"I'd just as soon not hear."

"I'm sorry."

Michael sat staring at his drink with a gloomy look on his face. Then he said, "I guess I'm lucky I called you now. I mean you wouldn't have wanted to go out with me if I'd called when you were – seeing someone."

"Oh, I don't know. You're pretty cute, you know."

"So it is physical," he said.

"What?"

"You were saying before, that with your old boyfriend it might have been just physical."

"No, what I said was that it was not necessarily just physical with you and your old girlfriend. And I was starting to say that with all the men I've seen since I broke up with my boyfriend, I've never been so really close to anyone." She smiled and looked up at him. "Though it certainly was physical, from the first day, and that's not my style."

"But was it mostly physical?"

"I miss him," she said. "I wish he would call me. A lot."

"You do?"

"I do."

"You could have called him."

"No, I did too much of that. I realized finally that if I didn't call him, that would be the end of it. He simply didn't care enough. So I swore that I wouldn't. And I haven't."

"He sounds like a pretty cold character."

"Yes."

"Well, you can't ever tell. Maybe one day when you least expect it, your phone will ring."

She gave a little smirk.

"Just as I called you out of the blue."

"I doubt it. It's been a long time now."

They were silent then, until Annie asked, "So was it very physical at the start with your old girlfriend?"

"She was a friend of a friend, so I was really not going to push anything, you know."

"Ah, so normally you would have?"

"Well – "

"Men."

"But – "

"All right, go on with this very amusing story."

"After dinner I figured we would go down to the Village and listen to music. Not push things. But she took it upon herself to suggest we go back to her place for coffee. Since it was right nearby, she said."

"Well, that sounds innocent enough. I believe her explanation. It doesn't mean she was coming on to you. She wanted to make you coffee."

"Yeah, she never even boiled the water."

"She didn't use a coffee maker?"

"No her method was pouring boiling water over a filter full of coffee. Very quaint."

"She intended to boil the water. She really didn't have anything in mind. She didn't usually sleep with a guy the first time. She just got carried away."

"You're speaking for her?"

"I can tell from what you said of her."

"Well, it may be. It was just amusing, that's all, that here I was for once trying to make a good impression and not come on strong, so she would know I was really interested. We were always at cross-purposes, it seemed. I used to kid her that maybe everything would have been different if she had only boiled the water."

"Do you think it might have?"

"No, of course not. It was just — our whole relationship was so neurotic, I think we both longed for something simple to pin all the illogic on. We both wanted it to work. We kept on trying long enough."

The food came, and for a while they ate without speaking. The moon appeared, a large crescent, and disappeared in low, fast-moving clouds. The breeze became brisk, balmy.

"Want a taste?" Annie asked.

Michael nodded.

"So let me ask you this," Annie said. "I'm not the first person you've gone out with since — since her, am I?"

"No, I've — I didn't go out with anyone for a long, long time, unlike you. Then I forced myself to meet someone. I couldn't stand the thought that my old girlfriend was probably fucking her ass off. It made me sick to think about it."

"She wasn't."

"After that, I met some women I actually liked."

"Oh, you did?"

"Well, I'll tell you this. I don't think there are a dozen days in the last two years I have not thought of, of her, my old girlfriend."

"Really? That's very sweet."

"Perhaps you will put that past out of my head."

"What if I bring it all back? The bad part?"

"No."

"No?"

"We started off wrong, my old girlfriend and I. If I were to get involved with you I would use what I've learned. I've thought about it. A real lot: I would make sure it was different. Not acting out self..."

"There goes the shrink talking again."

"Well, really, it's important."

"I don't know, Mickey. I really don't know. People are themselves."

Annie sat there shaking her head and peering into her water glass, and Michael found himself withdrawing inward.

"Life isn't good mostly, you know?" Annie said with a melancholy far-off sound in her voice. "Sometimes you try to kid yourself into thinking it can be."

"That is a pretty gloomy view. So why are you here?"

"Well, you, my old boyfriend, after him, I was looking for, for Mr. Esmond, just a nerd, an accountant type, who would be kind to me and put me on a pedestal and treat me like a queen."

"They're out there."

"Yes, they are."

"And?"

"I found them."

"So?" he said icily. "I repeat, why are you here?"

"It wasn't enough."

She looked at him and smiled. She put the bounce back in her voice when she spoke. "What do you do if one day when your life is way down in the dumps, out of the clear blue you meet the one person in the world you just know God absolutely made especially for you, out of all the thousands of people, the millions of people; every day the more you learn about him, the more you know it's true and the more incredible it seems that you stumbled across each other; only what do you do when you discover that despite being created by God to order for each other, you just can't seem to get along?" She looked at him hard, demanding an answer.

Then she started to laugh. It grew until she was holding her stomach, heaving with convulsive, painful laughter, and crying that she was going to throw up. Michael, attempting to keep the swaying glasses on the table, started to laugh then too. He saw the people at the next table smiling at them; then they too were laughing. Annie by now had her head in her lap, covered with the end of the tablecloth so she wouldn't see him.

When they were calm again, Michael paid the waiter with his card. Annie offered to pay half, but he refused. She was wiping the tears out of her eyes still. Across the table, his fingers touched hers. He took her hand and squeezed it. The fingers were thin and delicate. Her hand was warm in his. They gazed at each other, as she shook her head slowly back and forth, smiling like a mother at an incorrigible child.

"So what now?" he asked.

"I — don't — know," she sing-songed with a terrible frown and pout on her face.

The waiter returned with Michael's card, and he signed the slip.

"You could come over for coffee," Annie suggested.

They left the restaurant; it was cool in the summer night. Michael took her hand as they walked.

Annie opened her door carefully. The cat, she said, was like a cannon shot going out that door and would be four flights up before they had it fully open.

Inside, Michael sat on the couch and lifted Mr. Esmond, who perched calmly on his knee. Annie frowned as Michael gently scratched Mr. Esmond's chin. Mr. Esmond purred.

Annie plopped down in the corner of the couch and watched Mr. Esmond drifting into ecstasy as Michael scratched behind his ear. "He remembers you."

Abruptly, the cat dove for a fly that had squeezed through a crack in the screen.

"I'll put some music on," Annie said, lifting herself off the couch.

Michael took hold of her arm and pulled her down on his lap. Her gray blue eyes went up and down and sideways, taking in his face. "My own very own Mickey," she said, a tear welling out of the corner of one eye. Then she jumped up. "I still haven't bought a coffee maker. "Do you want decaf or regular? This may not have a prayer in hell, but I'm at least going to boil the water this time."

Still Life Of Melinda With Wildflowers

I T HAD BECOME A tradition that Melinda brought him flowers on the weekend. But in the last half year, as things
grew worse and worse between them, she often forgot. When
Lawrence said to her sadly on those occasions, "You never bring
me flowers now," she replied by singing the song *You Don't Bring
Me Flowers* in a deep chesty voice not at all like hers, and usually
he smiled.

Now that she was gone, he bought flowers himself, for their
beauty and for the tradition and for the sadness also. It was
nearly two months since they had gone through the motions of
pain yet another weary time, lashing out almost by rote. Both of
them saw with resignation that it was happening again and both
of them knew they had reached their limits of endurance.

Every moment of that night was vivid in his memory. Late
as usual, he was hurrying down Broadway looking for an open
florist. He felt expansive at the start of the evening, so he bought
big pink mums to surprise her with. She had been calling all day
making and changing plans and finally they decided to meet at
her office down on Church Street and walk over to Chinatown.

He was disappointed that he was late. He had wanted so
to surprise her by being on time. But she was resigned to

his lateness, and would be proven right again. Melinda, in a spring-white, calf-length skirt and burgundy sweater, looked very pretty. A smile of recognition when she saw him, an irrepressible smile, spread across her face. She flicked her curly brown hair. Stood up and strode toward him, hugged him while Lorraine put her coat on. Melinda told him pointedly that Lorraine waited so she wouldn't be alone in the office. Lawrence apologized, thanked Lorraine, started to chat with her. Just being polite. Sensed Melinda grow tense. Could hear Melinda in his head saying that he liked talking to Lorraine more than to her. Sensed that in the present sulfurous air any spark could touch off an explosion. So he stopped making conversation, and Lorraine hurried off. Melinda studied her watch, making a point; then she focused on the mums he had been holding all this time, and smiled.

Relief. They had made it past his lateness. He thought they had made it past Lorraine, too, but he was mistaken. On the way out, Melinda asked him, "Do you think Lorraine is prettier than me?"

"No," he said, feeling the weariness of climbing a mountain he had climbed before.

"But you think she's pretty, don't you?"

"She's not my type."

"You like them more whorey."

"I like them just like you."

"No really, I know your type." She trailed off, letting it go.

It was a cool night. They were on Worth Street just above Foley Square now. They had the street mostly to themselves. They stopped to decide whether they really wanted Chinese food or not. They considered going back to Brooklyn where she lived and having Italian food on Cobble Hill. Melinda didn't want her mums to be out of water too long, but they decided to go on to Mott Street after all.

A tall blonde with high cheekbones and a luscious mouth sauntered by. The blonde's steely blue eyes were fixed on Melinda and Lawrence teased her about it.

"I thought she was checking you out, actually," Melinda responded, and mused, "She was prettier than me."

Lawrence gave her a look.

"Darcy called today," he said. His friend Darcy had called just before he left to meet Melinda. That was why he was late. He always had a reason; he was not purposely late.

"Maybe you'll marry Darcy," Melinda said.

It exasperated him. What response could he give to that ludicrous statement that wouldn't set her off? He tried lightness. "I'd have to bump David off first, and he is huge."

"You'd be good together," she said thoughtfully.

Unlike us, he gathered she meant. "Why did you say that?" he asked. He stopped walking and leaned against the side of a building. Darcy had told him that when he saw they were descending into this absurd abyss, he should try to deconstruct the descent for Melinda, make her talk through each sentence that had gotten them to this place they did not want to be.

"Say what?"

"Why were you trying to make me feel guilty about Darcy? You must know that Darcy is not a threat to you. You do know that absolutely. I know you do. So why?"

She looked down at the ground, her mouth tightening. "You're causing trouble," she mouthed.

"That's not exactly fair."

"I just wanted to have a nice night, to have a nice dinner."

"But you didn't."

"All I said was —"

He rolled his eyes in frustration. He saw how frail his own control was. How they vibrated against each other.

"Goodbye, Lawrence. Thanks for the flowers. I can't take this tonight." She started to walk off.

He yelled after her, "Don't be melodramatic." She stopped, but didn't turn around. He walked up to her, still talking loudly though they were close.

"Don't yell at me," she said, and turned to him, her eyes filling.

"I'm not yelling at you," he yelled. And then he talked lower. "What was the point of that comment?"

She started to cry. "Don't you see what you're doing? I just wanted to have a nice little night. But you don't want to. You can't let anything go. You build it up into a mountain."

"I just want you to say you see, that you understand what you were doing."

"Lower your voice."

"Will you just listen to me."

"Not until you stop yelling at me."

"I'm not yelling. Why can't you listen to what I'm saying?"

"What do you want, Lawrence? I really don't know what you want."

"Why are you so stupid?"

"No, Lawrence, I'm not stupid. I'm not going to stand here and be yelled at. If I'm such an evil person, why don't you go and find someone else." She was crying again. "Why don't you just go. Just — go."

A family was walking their way. The three little children were holding hands. Lawrence watched the children's swinging arms. He looked up at Melinda's now icy eyes and the barely controlled rage in her rigid cheeks, and he turned and walked away. He felt the soft rustle against his back as the mums hit him. But he didn't turn. He just kept walking. He headed west.

He wanted Melinda to come running up and hold him, but of course she wouldn't. He walked half a block, and then glanced back. But she was not behind him. He turned north and walked up through TriBeCa, through the deserted cobblestone streets, by the dingy warehouses and lofts, and up to Canal Street, where the sudden glare and noise of traffic jarred him. He continued up through SoHo, passed the bars full of people and the closed galleries and boutiques with memories of happy, sauntering Saturday afternoons together.

In the Village, he walked into a burger place, and found himself flirting with the waitress. In revenge, he thought. He stopped talking to the waitress. He bit into his hamburger and chewed. Bit and chewed.

⸺◆⸺

As Lawrence lay in the bathtub in his brownstone apartment, thinking about Melinda, he could just see the yellow daisies in the vase on the end table in the living room and they made him feel sadder. She liked daisies especially. He swooshed the suds around and turned on the hot water with his toes. His cat was restless. She didn't like him staying in the water so long. When she got nervous, she ran a lot, and he could hear her on a tear from couch to rocker and back. He raised his leg, turning the hot off, and heard the noise of the rocker clanking dully back and forth. So many times it had ended with one of them stalking out. So many times they came back, desperate for each other.

He tried to think of the nice days, Melinda sitting on the floor of the bathroom draped in a towel while her hair dried. He saw her there propped up on a floppy pillow reading to him as he lay in the hot bath, his penis bobbing pink through the white soap bubbles: like a periscope; searching her out, he told her.

When Furball ventured in, craning her neck forward in apparent disbelief and stepping gingerly over sections of newspaper, patches of puddled floor, and glasses of vodka tonics in that slow-motion way cats have, Melinda stopped reading and spoke with the cat. The thrust of the conversation was a statement by Melinda of Furball's opinion that only a moron would cover himself with water. Lawrence smiled, shifting bubbles around. He leaned out of the tub to place a dab on Melinda's knee. Furball listened momentarily to the fizzing sound of the bubbles, then retreated with all the feline grace she could muster to the safety of the living room.

That was the night they had talked about getting season tickets to Triangle Stage. It was a kind of minor commitment to the future together. She joked about custody of the tickets, but in spite of everything, they both believed they would be together for the whole series. She had never wanted to hold her tickets; that was part of the faith.

There were four plays, eight tickets. The arithmetic of it was important, of course, only in the event of dissolution. They saw the first play during a good period. Two down, six to go. They patched up a bad break just in time to see the second play together. Four down, four to go. Halfway to a future that now looked as if it were not to be. The third play was still to come — on her birthday. And the fourth, he had just been advised, was being rescheduled. They were sending him new tickets for it (tickets seven and eight) for a date in August. He could not fathom getting from now to then in this life of his.

When he hoisted himself out of the tub, Lawrence turned on the stereo, and lay down on the couch. The bath had left him lethargic and drowsy. He must have fallen asleep because he was startled by the ringing of the telephone.

"Hello, it's Melinda," the voice said. Nausea rolled over his grogginess. Day after day he had longed for the telephone to ring. But her very first words turned him angry. He knew her name. He knew her voice. In good times, he picked up the receiver to find her already a sentence into her conversation. It stung, her telling him who she was.

The voice went on, "If you're not doing anything now —"

His heart skipped, but with her next words it sank. "I just wanted to stop off and pick —"

He hung up then, and after a minute lifted the receiver off the hook so she couldn't call again. The sentence was going to finish, "pick up my things," he was sure of it, and he could not face hearing that sentence.

The last time that one of them had stalked off, they had not spoken to each other for five weeks, and while they were trying to get used to its being over, they both felt the presence of her things in his closet, or, in his case, in the bags he had packed them in during his first fury. When finally she was back that time and saw her things all packed up in shopping bags, she laughed and said that when it was really over he could be sure she would not leave her things.

Furball sensed his tension and was crouching under the rocker staring at him, with her whiskers all pointing down. Why, he asked himself as he paced the room, did he feel so terrified? He tried to reason that they could not get along. It should be over. It was over. Her picking up her things was simply a burp at the end of a lousy meal.

When he was calmer, he knew he wanted to hear the words; he wanted the end to finally come and be explicit. So he called her back, jittery and cold. "What did you want before?" he asked her "Hello."

"I wanted to get my things."

The matter-of-fact calmness in her voice was excruciating for him.

"But I can't now. I have company. I'll have to call you back."

"Don't bother," he screamed. "You can get your fucking things whenever you want. They'll be outside the door. Good-bye!"

She was saying in that steady, I'm-not-upset-but-you-are voice, "Don't put them out until I'm ready to come," when he hung up.

In a fury he stormed around the apartment dumping everything of hers into a bag. First to the closet: the white frilly nightgown she liked to float around in on Sunday mornings doing pirouettes and plies with a cup of coffee in one hand. He yanked at the jeans that molded to her luscious body. The wire hanger spun off the rod and rattled to the floor. From his dresser he pulled the bottle of perfume that she never used but kept there because she liked to see a touch of herself among his things. From the bathroom, Tampax, face creams, cream for the diaphragm. He stared at the diaphragm as he replaying the phone call in his head. Was it only Anna or Donna visiting her? Why did she say "company"? More than anything, her calmness drove him.

When the bag was filled, he opened his door and dumped it in the hallway, slammed his door closed and walked through the apartment looking for anything of hers he may have forgotten. He collapsed into bed without bothering to undress. and pulled the covers up around his head. Overcome with a sudden drowsiness, he fell asleep.

When he awoke in the morning, he peeked out the door to see if the bag were still there. Every day when he came home from work his heart pounded as he climbed the stairs to his apartment. On the second day he added a note on a piece of scrap paper. "This is a sadness that will never heal. To know that you needed me as much as I needed you, and always will."

On the fourth day the bag was gone. There was nothing in its place. If she had just left a daisy, or a little freesia. Looking at the empty space which he had come to expect to see filled made her absence suddenly frightening and his emptiness enormous.

The last time they had gotten back together, when she called and listened to his silence for long minutes — he waiting for her to say something nice to him, she thinking he ought to say hello — she had finally said she was coming over. When she buzzed, he let her in. When they had hugged for an age, she said, "Ohhh, I haven't felt real all this time." He said that nothing had existed but emptiness, vast emptiness. She told him, "You know that you can't get rid of me. I'll always be here." He had been the one to leave that time. "You can't help yourself. Don't you see, it is silly to try to leave me? A wart with legs," she said. "Wherever you go the wart goes with you."

Now, he called Darcy to talk. Told her that they had broken up again. He had said it so often that she was careful this time. "I think it may be for the best," she said. He knew it was not for the best; it was simply to stop destroying each other.

"What do you fight about?" she asked him. He could not fathom it himself much less explain it to Darcy. And she refused to accept it when he told her they belonged together, that they were right for each other, had the same soul. "All you do is fight."

"No , you don't understand. We are so happy when we are together. I have never felt so content with anyone. It's just — "

"You just fight all the time."

"We can't seem to deal with —"

"You just fight all the time."

"I guess so."

"It isn't right then."

"But —"

"You fight all the time."

He was silent.

"There'll be someone else, you know. There always is."

The days passed. That first moment awakening in the morning was like sinking into a quagmire of suffocating darkness. But every time he was about to call her, he stopped himself. He knew neither of them could change the hysteria that gripped them, that blew them around, enveloped them. All they could do was batten down against the storm in their brains: it was like lightning slicing through the blackness ahead of the noise. Then came the noise. Then came the silence. Then the tears rained down. It was of the elements. They could not control it. And its ebb and flow shaped their relationship. Together they were like one grand mal seizure; the fit would run its course and there was nothing to do but — grit your teeth. One moment, they were hugging. The next:

"You might aim," she said half-jokingly as she walked into the bathroom where he stood.

"I'm trying," he said, bending down and wiping the floor. "It's hard with an erection."

"I never heard of any other adult man missing."

"You've never seen the floor of a men's room," he said, trying to keep it light.

"You think it's just a big joke, don't you?"

"Well, it is sort of funny."

"Damn you. God damn you. Would you just leave. Just go home." She was screaming now.

He started to dress. She watched, glaring at him, until he had his underpants and socks on and then she said with clenched teeth and fists, and cheeks drawn so tight that she looked as if she were ninety, "You bastard."

She ran around snatching up his pants and shirt and one shoe and locked them in her arms. "Don't you dare leave!" she shrieked.

He came after his clothes slowly and she dodged, but finally he got hold of a pant leg and pulled till the whole bundle fell loose. As he bent down to pick up his pants, she dove at him, bowling him over and pounding at him with her fists, pummeling him in the face and side, and biting his arm and screaming shrilly that she hated him. Caught off guard, he struggled with her weight on him. Finally gaining the leverage, he flipped her off and rolled on top of her. Then holding her down with his body and avoiding her flailing arms, he swung at her. The pain and the shock of being slapped frightened her and she stopped coming at him. As they lay there panting, his eyes tried to take in this frail, small bundle of fury and love and hate. His right cheek ached and burned where she had landed a punch.

When he let her up, she sat on her big stuffed chair with her hands folded in her lap staring at the floor for an endless time.

He stood and watched her from the middle of the room. She wouldn't look back. Finally he spoke. "I didn't miss on purpose." The words sounded inane. He choked back tears.

She looked up at him finally out of big pleading, despairing eyes. Suddenly, she began crying a flood of hysterical tears and gasping out gloomy words about how evil she was and about not deserving to live, and asking him in a seductive whisper to help her do herself in. "I wanted to pulverize you," she hiccoughed out. "How could I hit you? How could I do that?"

⸻ ◆ ⸻

Her birthday came. He dreaded the day; he longed for the day. Maybe this was when she would call. He meant to go out and do something, anything. But he couldn't pull himself away from the telephone. He lay in his bed, staring at the ceiling, waiting. Thinking the day would never end; watching the hours fly away. The phone never rang. Maybe, it occurred to him, she expected him to call her for her birthday. He thought about what was stopping him. He came up blank.

Darcy drove down that evening to mother him, and they went to the play. He noted that they were using numbers five and six, of course, so seven and eight, the tickets for the rescheduled play, when they came, would by all rights belong to Melinda. The last vestige of her property that he held.

As the weeks continued to roll by, the ringing of the telephone, which had bored into his stomach and set his palms to sweating, began to lose its power. And then one Saturday in June soon after the mail had brought the new tickets for the last play at Triangle Stage, the call came.

"Hello, it's Melinda."

He was not prepared. He was silent. Tried to intuit from the tone of those three words what was in store.

"How have you been?" she asked.

Clarity. Her name. The attempt at conversation. The tone. It was that tone that said "we're two mature people and even if it didn't work out, it isn't the end of the world." Something collapsed in him. He didn't have the control to continue this conversation long enough to determine whether she was over him, in fact, or putting a face on her pain. He had been strung tight too long. The indifference in her voice loosed a fury.

"Damn you," he said. "Don't try to be civilized. Don't you understand how much I hate you?"

"Lovely," she said, not even modulating her cool. "Well, you won't be thrilled with this, then. I was looking at the paper and I saw the ad for the new play at Triangle. Don't I have some tickets coming to me?"

"Right, I kept them to cheat you."

"Well they sure were not in with my things. Draw your own conclusions."

"You've already drawn yours. You'll get your tickets," he said, and he slammed down the phone.

He sat with the tickets in his hand for a long time, reciting the seat number and section and performance date in his head monotonously. August twenty-seventh.

Next morning, a sunny, crisp, breezy morning of vivid shadows and darting light, Lawrence, holding an envelope, stood in front of a mailbox. With butterflies beating their wings tremulously in his depths, he opened the box and slid the tickets in.

He had hoped for some response, but now it was August; summer had come and was going and he had not heard a word. He sat with a mug of steaming coffee this early morning, alone on the back terrace of Darcy and David's house upstate. In the window boxes that ringed the terrace, the still dew-flecked petals of white impatiens, delicate and pure, glowed alongside the marigold clumps of rust and amber intimating autumn. Flowers had been such a part of his time with Melinda that being surrounded by flowers now brought a sudden outpouring of tears.

A bumblebee made its rounds of the window boxes on the lattice brick wall of the terrace. Beyond, the trees rustled in the cool breeze. A plane droned overhead. Lawrence flicked carelessly at his damp cheek as the bee hovered, then lowered itself into the cup of a creamy impatiens, barely touching the flower, then darting off and dropping into a fold of marigold; and another and another; veering, swerving; busily, ceaselessly at its work.

Darcy popped out the back door, in her pink bathrobe, singing, "Good morning, Lawrence," her long, yellow hair flowing as she shook her head and raised her arms into the air, stretching and yawning. "Oh, it's a glorious day, isn't it? How are you? Thank you for making coffee. Are you hungry yet? David is going to make his special Sunday breakfast."

"I can eat any time," Lawrence said.

"Oh good."

"Is it a surprise, David's dish?"

"It's an omelet like you never tasted. Come have some strawberry bread." Lawrence started to get up. "No, stay. I'll bring it out." When she reappeared, a vision in pink and yellow, she carried a tray with the loaf, and butter and plates. David, a craggy towering image, said good morning. They went at the bread earnestly, and then David returned to the kitchen to cook. Darcy brought the paper out for Lawrence and a pile of her work to wade through. "Oh, we're so glad you're here," she said. "We've missed you a whole bunch."

Lawrence smiled. He looked for the bumblebee, but it was gone. Gazing out over the yard with far-away eyes, he saw himself with Melinda the summer before in a field that was painted blue and lavender with wildflowers. They sat on a low, flat rock and his hand rested on her thigh. He wore cut-offs, a tee shirt and sneakers. All around his bare legs the bees toiled. More than he could count. As Melinda's voice melded with their buzzing, he watched the tiny striped bodies dance. They flitted close at times, but he just knew they would not sting.

Melinda was reading to him. Her voice was small in the open air, but strong and happy. In her curly, brown hair, two yellow flowers began to droop as her reading became dramatic and her head bobbed. He leaned toward her, pushing the stems back into the tangled curls. She paused in her reading and they kissed.

Each morning of that trip, when they walked in the still forest, he picked her a different color wildflower for her hair. He had come to look forward to finding the perfect flower for each morning's mood. She felt silly at first; when they passed people, she would pull the flower out. He pouted when she did that. Then, when one morning he forgot to pick her a flower for her hair, she pouted.

Lawrence glanced over at Darcy who sat with her coffee mug in her hand, reading. Then he gazed back out over the trees and garden. It had been growing on him for about a week now, since August had come; a feeling at first, just a vague feeling. But more and more each day, a hope, and sometimes in his thoughts, a certainty. He kept remembering her telling him, "Don't you see, whatever our problems are, we belong to each other. You'll never be able to keep me away. The wart with legs. Always with you. You're mine. I'm yours."

He realized he was living for August twenty-seventh, that last theater date. Every day he was more and more sure that he knew what her gesture would be. Every day he came home from work expectantly, hurrying to open the mailbox, and when he found nothing there, hurrying to open his door, peering down at the floor to see if an envelope with a little ticket had been slipped under.

And often, lying in bed, he fantasized the scene as he knew it would happen. He would come late just before the curtain. From a distance he would see her sitting there already, with the empty seat beside her, darting eyes searching for him. He would sit down and start to read his program, but they would both be unable to hold back the grins of happiness and they would hold hands, squeezing hard. And then the play would start.

The omelet was every bit as good as Darcy had promised. They were a happy couple, Lawrence thought, Darcy and David, in their airy, neat, plant-filled house. Darcy said the peppers and scallions in the omelet were from the garden. David told him how many tomatoes they had had to put up, and finally just give away. "There's a limit to how much two people can consume."

After breakfast, Darcy perked fresh coffee.

"She buys this much Colombian and that much Brazilian and a pinch of Chilean — the mountain air, you know. I think she's crazy, but you have to humor them." David stood and strode over to Darcy, who was standing with her mug. He straddled a chair and pulled her down on his lap. She was laughing and holding the mug out trying to keep it from spilling as he clamped his huge hands around her shoulders and massaged the muscles.

They walked in the woods after breakfast. It was already getting hot, but under the rustling trees it was cool.

One summer morning, Lawrence had awakened at five-thirty. Melinda slept against him, so he didn't move. But unable to fall back asleep, he thought he would go for a walk in the dawn. He managed to extricate himself without waking her, quickly dressed and tiptoed out, closing the door softly behind him and carefully locking it. He padded down to the park and walked along the river, feeling happy and at peace. A light mist hung over the water. Far up, the bridge was shrouded in fog. The ground was still puddled from rain during the night, and the fishy smell of the water mingled with the damp, dank smell of the earth.

He listened for a long time to the waves lapping against the rocks, and then he began to notice the wildflowers scattered so randomly everywhere. He set about picking a bouquet for

Melinda. He got caught up in the effort, searching for new shapes, new tones among the delicate, fragile bits of color. Pleased with himself when he counted nine different kinds of flowers and half a dozen different ferns in his bouquet, he hurried home and tiptoed in.

She slept still, on her side, almost on her stomach, her hair fallen over her face. Laying the bouquet down on the pillow close against her cheek, he sat behind her and waited.

Eventually she awoke, muttering his name in a sleepy garble, and moving her arm to push the hair out of her face. She realized in a hazy half-sleeping way that something was there that didn't belong, and she squinted through her hair at it, coming slowly awake.

He could see her face melting into a smile as she recognized the bouquet and began looking around for him. When she found him, she reached out and hugged him. Then she jumped out of bed and danced around the sun-drenched apartment, holding her bouquet to her breast, stopping now and again to gaze in the mirror at still life of Melinda with wildflowers, as she put it.

By afternoon the flowers, resting now in a vase, were wilted. A tear rolled down her cheek as she threw the bouquet away; it was a tear of happiness. She kissed him, and rested her head against his chest.

Unresolved Sexual Tension

"**C**AN I DREDGE UP *l'affaire* for a minute? Do you mind?"

"Why? That was eons ago, Lila. I haven't seen him in forever. We talked it to death — how do you lawyers say it? — 'contemporaneously.'"

"Lawyer by marriage. I know. I'm just curious about certain things. Brad's not home, is he?"

"No."

Lila, her phone on speaker, lay back, propped on a pillow on the arm of the sofa. "Are you sure Brad never had any suspicions? Never found out?"

"No of course not. Lila. Lila? Why are you asking this now? I was incredibly careful." Lola started to laugh.

"Did you worry about it at the time? That he might find out. That maybe he knew, but was not saying anything; didn't want to stir up a hornet's nest? What's so funny?"

"If he did, I would be a fucked, impoverished, lonely old lady. Shit, Lila, you didn't let something slip, did you? After ten years."

"No, of course not. You don't know it would have been like that. Brad loves you."

"Not enough to forgive *that*." Lola fell silent.

Lila rearranged the pillow under her head. She realized that Lola would get the point of these questions before much longer and decided she was not ready to provide a big reveal today. Not that the reveal was very big.

"Lila!" came the blast of exclamation. And then a very slow, "Lila, what — are — you — telling — me? Is there something you wish to share, sweetheart?"

Lila smiled. After forty-eight years they knew each other too well. Lola, Lila, and Lorna, the Three L-sketeers from the dorm freshman year in college. "I think not," Lila said. "Bye bye." She gently hit the disconnect button. "No dear," she said to her living room, "nothing I wish to share today." Trixie, her cockapoo, looked up briefly, apparently agreed, and so went back to sleep.

She thought about the day last week that she sent the email. Bernie had risen at 5:30, was off for his precious round of tennis with Dexter by 5:45. He showered at the courts after the game, as he did every morning. Called her from the office at three, as per their routine. Home for dinner at seven. She had cooked a really nice stuffed flounder. He was pleased. In his quiet way he got excited about food. "Remarkable," he said. "Is that turmeric?"

"Uh huh."

He picked up a last forkful and savored it; squeezing her hand. It was as domestic and ordinary a day as it could be.

But sometime before the flounder hit the oven, sometime in the afternoon, after calling her architect about the gut of one of the upstairs bathrooms that was on her definite list for this summer, she did the deed.

Why had she even thought of him? She was quite sure as she now considered it that her intent had been totally innocent. The day's mail had brought her a solicitation from the college. She always gave a little. As she sat on her deck with her checkbook, daydreaming about those long ago days, she conjured the places imbued with memories, eventually coming to the elegant library reading room redolent of waxed wood, pools of light from brass lamps on the polished study tables, hushed voices. He had floated into her mind then, and with her curiosity aroused, she did a search. For all she knew, he might be dead. She was sixty-six, so he would be close to seventy. Once she thought about that, the whole thing became ludicrous. What would they possibly have to say to each other? Lipitor vs. Crestor. Amlodopine vs. Valsartan. They were senior citizens; crap, they were friggin' old; elderly; aged. What was she thinking?

There he was. He had been a teacher, not surprisingly. Some college she never heard of. Now retired, apparently. He seemed to have something to do with real estate these days. No good photos; fuzzy, dark. Nothing recent at all.

She remembered him as very nice looking in a plain way. Not a hunk or a chiseled face you would notice immediately. Thin. Long hair. Everyone had long hair then. No one was bald yet then either. Bernie had curly red hair, almost like a long Afro. He started losing it in his late thirties. Another decade and he was basically bald. For a while now, Bernie had been shaving his head. She had never minded his baldness. Anyway, she was used to it.

She could hardly complain. Her face was getting — a prune came to mind, well not that bad. In her opinion, a few wrinkles gave her character. After a party they had thrown last weekend for his partners and others, Bernie told her someone from the firm she did not know had commented to him that his wife looked beautiful — elegant and beautiful, he had said. "Such a good feeling knowing we have always been able to have absolute faith in each other," Bernie had added as an afterthought. They kissed.

"It is wonderful," she agreed.

Devin. Thin. Wry, actually quite funny. His subtle wit was what had attracted her in whatever way she was attracted to him. The truth was she could not remember quite what her feelings were toward him, except that they were good friends for a period. It was not sexual. Bernie was the third and last person Lila had ever had sex with. She was an anachronism even then.

They chatted in the library; had coffee here and there around campus. At one point, she seemed to remember, they took a drama workshop together. Not that any of it was clandestine. She had readily told Bernie about him at the time. After she graduated and got married, she was never on campus. It had been a casual friendship, and they never saw each other again. But she remembered him after forty-five years. And if she were truthful, he had popped into her head on and off over the decades. Fleeting thoughts. What if she had not been engaged when they met? What would her life have been like with him? Wispy thoughts over the years that blew away as quickly as they materialized. But now it was more than a wispy mist.

"Hi, I'm sure you probably don't remember me. I mean it's only been forty-five years! We met in the Library's Silent Reading Room when I was in college and you were in graduate school. My roommate had you in class and I came up to your table to ask you when you were teaching that class again. We weren't exactly silent. The librarian kept giving us daggers. Remember her? Ha Ha. We talked till the room closed. 'Half hour before library closing,' remember? 'Strictly adhered to.' We became friends. Just thought about you for some reason, and wondered how you are doing. Assuming of course that you are still alive. Ha Ha. Hope to hear from you (even more interesting if it's from beyond the grave.)

Your friend, Lila Ezekiel."

After she hit the send button, she was on pins and needles. She did not hear back that day, or the next or the next. Maybe it was stupid to put in that bit about 'beyond the grave.' She sounded like a goofy twenty-year-old. It was not at all funny. Honestly, she was just as happy he had not responded. Maybe he was actually dead.

Well, he wasn't dead.

"To the best of my recollection, I never knew a Lila Ezekiel." That was all he wrote.

She was surprised at how deflated she felt. He didn't remember her and he was not even curious. It hurt, which was ridiculous. She was glad that he didn't remember her. It had been a stupid idea. What would she even have said to him? Still, she was in a foul mood when Bernie came home after his weekly evening of doubles.

"Hello Trixie," Bernie said, scratching the dog's neck. "Why does mommy have such a sour look on her face? Humm?"

"The dinner will be cold."

"I'm sorry, darling. We were tied and the tie breaks just kept going on and on."

"Whatever."

Bernie was asleep and she was in bed beside him, browsing her I-Pad, answering mail, when the second email appeared: one of those emojis of a laughing face, laughing so hard it's eyes were tearing.

What the hell. What did he think was so funny? She had a momentary chill. She considered waking Bernie and telling him what she had done. But she just lay there staring at the new white floral curtains she had recently put up. Bernie had not noticed them. If she had hung tennis rackets he might have noticed.

Hard on the heels of that email came a third. "I did however know a Lila Berlin, and I remember her vividly."

She felt like a complete idiot. She had signed the email with her married name. Of course he wouldn't recognize it. What a doofus she was. He was laughing at her. He obviously searched Lila Ezekiel and found lots of references to Lila Berlin Ezekiel. Her whole body grew warm. She threw the blanket off and still she got warmer. It took her a minute to realize she was experiencing pure sensual excitement, a feeling quite unfamiliar in recent decades, recent millennia. "I remember her vividly." She read it again. "I remember her vividly." Bernie started snoring. She gave him a gentle elbow. He turned on his side, and his breathing grew quiet. She lay there, eyes wide open. "I remember her vividly."

⸺◆⸺

Lunch with Lorna at Daisy this late spring day. Bright and full of the promise of summer, though still a bit of a chill in the air. Lila came from exercise class. It had been their Wednesday morning thing, but Lorna was no longer participating in the class since her recent knee replacement. Lorna had already ordered the wine when Lila pulled the door open, nodded to James, the too-handsome by far young maitre d', and strode in.

Lorna was at their usual table by the window, her face half hidden by a lush vase overflowing with white daisies. "Goods, how was class? Am I missed?"

"*Comme toujours. Pas vraiment.* How's the knee?" Lila was struck by Lorna's gray hair. She had cut it short and had not bothered to color it blonde since her operation. Lila still could not get used to it. Lorna looked so old as a gray lady. She shuddered to think what she herself would look like gray. She kept her hair shoulder length, flipped at the bottom, an auburn color that Houston, her hairdresser, gushed was perfect for her. It was.

"Physical therapy is a bitch."

"Sorry."

Lorna shrugged it off as of no consequence. "So my darling," she said, raising her glass toward Lila, "Let's not beat around the bush."

"Oh, God, you talked to Gets."

"Indeed I did. Not that she knew much." Lorna gave her a long appraising look.

"Fuck."

"Really, already? That's not what you gave Gets reason to think."

"Oh stop. It's nothing like that. Do you remember back in college you had this English class with a TA you really liked? I can't remember what class it was."

"No. Who remembers TAs?"

"You really liked him. You told me to take the class. His name was Devin Remson."

"No. Sorry."

"You were not around much senior year. I never took the class or anything, but he and I became friends."

Lorna raised her eyebrows.

"Just friends. But I really liked him."

"And this is going where?"

"I don't know. I did something really, really unlike me. I don't even have a clue why." She told Lorna the story.

Lorna had a scolding look on her face. Her face was lean, the skin leathery and lined, and the scolding look made her thin lips thinner, her face pinched and tight. She was shaking her head.

"This is not what you want to do. You have a good marriage. One of the few. Let it go. Where is he, anyway?"

"Charlotte, North Carolina, maybe. Somewhere around there. Not that far from Lola actually."

"Even if it were not an incredibly stupid thing for you to get involved in, think of the logistics. And dare I ask, how old would he be? He is probably decrepit. What are you thinking?"

"So would you say we are decrepit, Doone? Huh?"

Lorna carefully lowered her leg from the chair on which she had been resting it. "In truth, I do feel quite decrepit. Sorry to say. But that doesn't mean you should take up with some old codger who can't get it up anymore."

"Thank you for sharing that, but *I* do not feel decrepit at all. I go to exercise class, I lift weights, I run five miles most every day, I walk Trixie. And I am sure he is in great shape, including his — his organ. Christ, Doone, I just want to talk to the guy on the phone. What is wrong with that? Why are your panties in a bunch?"

"Let it go. You don't want to do this, you really don't. You know it too, or you would not be asking."

"I do. I do want to!" Lila surprised herself by her vehemence. Until that moment, she had not known how strongly she felt about it.

⸻ ⬥ ⸻

"Sorry to hear you're not dead," she typed. "Would have been so interesting to know what it is like up there, or down there, in your case. Couldn't find recent pictures on line. Do you have hair?"

"Where?"

"Ha ha."

She waited, but he was gone.

Next morning, Lila was mindlessly straightening pictures on the mantle: her daughter, Diane, as an infant, as a toddler, Diane at her college graduation. Lila had her phone in one hand, checking emails as she straightened.

An email appeared. "Is the picture of you and him all dressed up recent? Accurate?"

She knew which picture it was. It was a portrait, a heavily touched-up portrait — her skin like a baby's — taken for a brochure her husband's law firm put out for some reason. It was a stretch to say that was what she looked like. "Yes."

"I'd love to see a picture from back then."

"I'd love to see a picture of you now," Lila said.

"Well, I looked a bit better then. A wee bit."

"Now and then, how about?"

"I'll look. And how about sending me something less formal from now." He wasn't stupid.

⚊⚊◆⚊⚊

Lola was in hysterics. Phlegmy hysterics. Lila could imagine her too-much belly and too many chins jiggling as she coughed and laughed and cradled the phone. When she stopped laughing and coughing, she said, "Nothing changes. It is all about the pictures. Sixty-six years old and all anyone wants is to see if the other person has some modicum of sex appeal left in the ravaged remains of a lifetime. He looks good, I have to say. Damn, honey, I wish this was happening to me! Did you show Doone?"

"No, Lorna does not approve."

"Oh, la, la. Ignore her. Just be verrry discrete."

"I am not doing anything. I have not even spoken a single word to the guy!"

"La la."

<hr>

"Oh, yes," he wrote. "That is exactly how I remember you. You were so so cute."

She studied the picture she had sent him. Her long, curly brown, shapeless hair tumbling down below her shoulders. Her face was round and pudgy. "I look fat. Butterball. It's the only picture I could find."

"You look adorable.Delectable."

"I would say 'thank you,' but that is 'looked,' forty-five years ago."

"You look good now too." She had sent him a recent snapshot that was not too sharply focused.

She could not think about much else as she went through her usual day. When Bernie came home, she could not wait till the next morning when he would go back to work.

"I think we should talk, don't you?" Devin wrote the next day. "Email has it's limits. Do you work? Any time is good for me."

Somehow, as innocent as that email was, it felt like an escalation. Her armpits were wet. Her heart was racing. She could not remember a rush like she was feeling.

At the time they agreed on, her phone rang. She felt a wave of dizziness. She lifted her phone and sat down hard on the couch. "Hello." Her voice sounded to her as if it were far away. She swallowed.

"Hi there."

His voice, in those two brief words, sounded so familiar; brought his whole being back to her.

"I'm good. How have you been?" He hadn't asked how she was, she realized. She sounded like an idiot, responding to a question not asked.

"You mean 'been' for the last forty-plus years? Would you prefer a mean or an itemization of the ups and downs?" He laughed. "A long time since our most recent meeting...." He paused briefly as if considering how to finish the sentence. "When you abandoned me to marital bliss."

"We were friends," she mumbled a protest.

"I'm glad you emailed me," he said.

"You are?"

"Yeah, I am. So tell me all about your last forty-five years."

Those first fifteen unbearably awkward seconds passed. Then she looked out the window and saw Bernie pulling into the driveway and realized four hours had disappeared. It was as if they had just talked the day before, had not been separated by four decades. By a lifetime of marriage and kids and jobs and illnesses and crises. "I guess I should go," she said. "My husband just came home and I have not even thought about dinner."

They talked every day. Their conversations went on for three and four hours in the morning. Then they emailed or texted until one of them felt the need to call again, yacking away until Bernie came home. An entire week went by like that. Then a second.

Their conversations were bantering and intimate, free-wheeling and not inhibited by the polite constraints of social discourse. Not like any conversations she ever had with Bernie.

"So tell me," he said, "do you fake orgasms or have them, or not have them but not fake them?"

"All of the above."

"Well, I don't want you to fake them with me."

"Aren't you forgetting one little thing?"

"What's that?"

"We're platonic friends."

"Oh, right."

Lila dreaded the weekends when it was difficult to talk. For the first time she was overjoyed that Bernie spent his weekend mornings at the tennis club.

<hr>

"He's really interesting, Lola. His idea of retirement is flipping houses. He didn't have a lot of money. He was a college teacher, but he bought this old divided-up house near campus and rented it out to students. Then when prices started going up, he sold it for a bunch, bought another one and sold it right away, and just kept going. Fun to him is open houses, chatting with real estate agents."

"Weird guy."

"No he isn't."

"Next thing he'll be buying in Harrisburg."

"You think that didn't come up?"

<hr>

He wanted to see her.

"That is not possible, realistically. You know that, right?"

"Then what is this about?"

"It is not about anything. We're friends. We have rekindled our friendship."

"I don't think that is exactly the way it is. To be honest, you're the one who got away."

"That is flattering."

"It's true. If I could have stolen you I would have. I tried. Don't you remember?"

"I was engaged. It was never about that. Don't *you* remember?"

"I remember very well. I remember that little glittering diamond."

She instinctively glanced down at her finger. Still there, still glittering. It was indeed little; all Bernie could afford. He offered to replace it later, when he could afford much better. But this was the only ring she wanted.

"You may have been engaged, but you were tempted. And it would have happened except I got sick. You finally finally agreed to come to my place to have dinner. Come on, you know what was going to happen that night. We both knew it. But I got sick and had to cancel, and then the moment passed. Why did you call me? Out of the blue? Why?"

"I told you..."

"Yeah, yeah. Just a hello to an old friend, right. Here's what I think." She heard a playfulness in his voice, but also an intensity.

"Yeah? Tell me oh wiser one than I."

"Three words."

"Can't wait."

"Unresolved sexual tension."

"What?"

"You heard me. It was there the whole time, from the moment you picked me up."

"I didn't pick you up."

"Uh huh."

"I really wanted you to be my teacher."

"Yeah, and I wanted to be your teacher!"

"Very funny. 'Unresolved sexual tension,'" she repeated. "I don't think so."

He went on. "I know so, and now..."

"Now what?"

"A resolution might be quite nice." He laughed. "We can't live in this fantasy land. I want to be with you in person."

She did not know how to respond. Be with me how? She stood up and walked into the kitchen, poured herself a glass of wine.

"Are you there?"

"I love our world," she finally answered. "It is not a fantasy. It is a private compartment of my life that you and I share. That is all it can be, so let's enjoy it for what it is."

———◄○►———

"He wants to see me."

"Naturally he does."

"You don't understand, we are on the phone or texting all day long." Lila was at Daisy with Lorna, in their usual seats.

"How do you know he is not married?"

"I'm married."

"Correct, let's dwell on that."

"He's divorced a long time. He told me and I checked that out. Two kids in their thirties, boy in New York, married; girl in Chicago, single. He's had girlfriends, but not now. Not for a while. It's hard to meet people at our age. I can see that."

"Yeah, hasn't he heard of swipe left, or is it swipe right? Or maybe the one for seniors would be better for him. Why don't you just tell him it's nice to talk to him again, but since he seems to want more than just reminiscing about old times, and you're happily married, you think you should not continue."

Lila hesitated, playing with her glass of wine. "The thing is, he's..."

"What?"

Lila covered her face with her hands and whispered, "Perfect."

"Oh God. Mr. Perfect."

"Was Bernie perfect? I don't even remember how I felt."

"Bernie was inevitable."

Was he? She thought about that dinner that never happened.

———◆○◆———

"Bernie is exercising. I can talk for a while."

"He's home? Are you crazy? You shouldn't be talking when he's home."

"We are not doing anything I should hide, are we? We are old friends talking on the phone. I am not doing anything wrong."

"Have you told him about our 'private world?'"

"No."

"Where is he exactly?"

"He is in the exercise room on a treadmill. He is nowhere nearby."

"Sound carries"

"Even if he walked in here, and stood right over my shoulder."

"He might get suspicious."

"You don't understand. Bernie is clueless. If it doesn't bounce, he is oblivious."

"It is not good."

"Trust me."

"Call me when he's not home. Even if, as you insist, this is perfectly innocent, even if, as you claim, there is no unresolved sexual tension, things can be misunderstood. You have much to lose."

"Ah, you're sweet. So protective. What if I want to lose it?"

"What?

"You heard me. I have too much to lose, you said. What if I want to lose it?"

"Is that what you want?"

"You said I was the one who got away."

"Don't you think we should meet maybe once before we make a final final decision?"

"Ha ha. Just thinking out loud, spinning webs."

—◦—

Lila was telling Devin about her day. "Bernie and I went out for ice cream, strolled along the Susquehanna, down between the Reading train bridge and the I-83 bridge. It was a beautiful day here. Gorgeous sunset. We watched it over dinner at an Indian place."

Devin was silent for a long time. "What's wrong?" she asked.

"Nothing. Nothing, I guess. It took me by surprise. I just didn't think of you going out for ice cream together. Not that you shouldn't. Were you holding hands?" he joked.

"Yes."

"Oh."

"Oh?" she said. "I do have a real life, you know. I have an actual relationship with my husband, a forty-seven-year relationship. I think that's the correct number."

Several moments passed. She wondered what he was thinking. Was he about to ask if they slept together? "I think it is best that we not talk about my husband at all. What I do with him is totally separate from you and me."

"You're right. I'm sorry. It is none of my business."

"It feels strange. I am living two separate lives. I love my husband. Nothing has changed. It's just that I have this other life. I, I love you too." She had not meant to say that, but it was what she felt, and it slipped out. She hurried on. "It is crazy. We don't even know each other. This has been all of three weeks."

"But we do really know each other, don't we?" Now he hesitated. "And it is what we both feel."

Lila thought for a moment. How to express this. "But it is all theoretical, isn't it? That's not the right word, but you know what I mean. We're old, Devin. Meeting in person could be a very rude awakening." She was wandering around the house and stopped in front of a mirror. Grimaced.

"You're making exactly my point. We have to meet in person. Or we're kind of floating in nowhere land."

"Fantasy land sounded better."

Lila was pacing. She started counting her steps. She walked upstairs, examined the bathroom she wanted redone. But her mind was elsewhere. She had made clear to Devin that their fantasy world had boundaries. It would not drift into the real world. She had said that. Over and over. Hadn't she? Bernie would be in Philly for two days. Leaving Wednesday, coming back early Friday. She impulsively picked up her phone. "I'm going way out of my box," she typed. "Can we meet for dinner Thursday? Somewhere in between." She thought for a moment she was having a heart attack. She lay down.

Then he texted. Then she texted. In the end, they realized it was not realistic. Too rushed. Too many difficulties. But she knew that text changed everything.

"The truth is you should just come to Harrisburg. That would be so much easier."

"What, are you crazy? That is the last thing we should do. Too many chances of someone in your web of social activities seeing us. No way. That is the one place I am not going. And as far as driving eight hours for, what, lunch...."

"You could meet Trixie. For that matter, you could have dinner with us."

"Dinner with your husband?"

"Why not? You'd like each other. It is perfectly natural. You and I are friends; what's wrong with that? We have a guest bedroom. You could stay with us."

"Me thinks there is a tad bit of miscommunication here."

⚬

"In the middle of July, Bernie has a bar function in Pittsburgh," Lila blurted out when he called. "He will be away for two weeks. Maybe then. I could say I am going to visit Lola since he will be away." She became aware that she was sitting up stiffly in the chair and her fist was clenched. She closed her eyes and pressed the lids tight. Neither of them spoke for a yawning several seconds. "Doone is going to freak about this," she mumbled.

"Doone? Who the hell is Doone?"

"My friend Lorna, you know, the one who took your class. The one who set us up, ha ha."

"Set us up? You picked me up."

"I did not."

"Right. Lorna Doone? You have got to be kidding."

"It's not her real name. Like we call Lola 'Gets.'"

"G-E-T-Z?"

"No, G-E-T-S"

"Gets?"

"You're smart, Dr. Professor. Figure it out."

"Lola Gets? Huh? Lola Gets. Lola Gets. Oh, I gets it. As in *Damn Yankees?*"

"Very good! What — ever — Lola — wants —"

"Oh please, don't sing. So what's your name?"

"I don't have one."

"How likely is that?"

"Well, what if I don't feel like telling you?"

"Come on."

"It's embarrassing. These names were just between us. Not for outsiders."

"I'm an outsider?"

"Well, duh." Lila sighed. "All right, Goods. You figure it out."

"You give the goods? Not to me, you didn't."

"Ha, hardly. Like just the opposite, as in Goody Goody. It was originally Goody; over the years turned into Goods." She laughed. "Does not quite fit at this moment, does it?"

Devin was silent.

"Hello."

"I'm here." But he remained silent for a time. He finally said, "This July thing, I just want to be clear. This is more than lunch, or dinner, we're talking about now?"

Lila took a deep breath. The word did not come out at first. She knew she should say, "Let's see how it goes."

"More," she said.

"I want you to come to North Carolina."

She thought all day about that. What if she did go, and their meeting went really badly? What if they were not attracted to each other? She would be stuck in his house. Far from home. So awkward. Anyway, July was too far off. Neither of them could go on like this. Something had to happen.

Frustrated, she wrote him, "Listen, if you want to see me, just come to Harrisburg any time you want. That is it. Period. It is up to you. Two or three days will be enough for a first time. During the week. I can't spend the nights, but we can have all day. The ball is in your court." Shit, she thought, I can't believe I used that expression.

⎯⎯◆⎯⎯

"News, News, News," Lila said, barely catching her breath as she sat down at Daisy.

"I'm all ears."

"Wait," she said, grabbing her phone, "Let me do video with Lola, so you can both hear."

Lorna sat back and sipped her drink.

"Gets? I'm here with Doone."

"Hi girls."

"She has something to tell us about Mr. P.," Lorna said.

"OK. I'm all ears."

"That's what I said."

"What, do you have a patent?"

"That would be copyright," Lila said. "As I've told you many times, I'm a lawyer by marriage. Anyway, Devin."

"Please: Mr. P."

Lila ignored her. "He's coming to Harrisburg. It's happening. Still working on details. I wanted him to come to my house the last day. He went berserk."

"Are you totally off your gourd?" Lorna said.

"I want to show him where I live, and Trixie."

"And fuck in your bed, Bernie's bed? And have someone see you together? And he'll forget some incriminating belonging of his. Yeah, great idea."

Lola lay on her couch laughing throughout this exchange.

"Well, it is not happening. Or, at least, we'll see."

"Ugh."

"His coming to Harrisburg should be safe. We won't have to go out at all. He made reservations at the suites place, avec kitchen. I want to cook for him."

"You want safe, here is my advice, honey," Lola said. "Take it from a gal with experience. Number one, do not use your credit card even once, anywhere, for anything. Number two, no photos."

"Make him use a condom," Lorna put in. "I know you. You are too trusting. You don't really have the remotest idea where his little member has been."

"La la la," Lola interrupted. "Membership does have some privileges, to paraphrase the commercial."

"I hope you are sure about this," Lorna said.

"You want to know the truth, I am scared to death. Standing in front of the mirror I almost backed out. I am a hag. My face is so old looking — have you actually looked at me lately? He's going to take one look and get back on the road."

"Well, that was not what I meant, as you very well understood, but if he does turn around and leave, you will know that about him. Maybe that would be the best outcome."

"Oh leave the girl alone," Lola said.

"OK, I'm about two hours away. Traffic's not bad at all."

"Oh my God, I can't believe this is really happening."

"I know. Four weeks. It has only been four weeks. Or is it going on five?"

"Four. I'm sixty-six years old. Oh my God. I'm doing this. I never had an affair before."

"It's fine. It'll be fine."

"Where are you?"

"Not sure. Less than two hours away."

"Text me when you get there. What if we see each other and one of us wants to vomit?" she asked.

"Well, let's both bring basins."

⸻◈⸻

The next morning was not like any morning in Lila's memory. When Bernie arose, she pretended to be asleep. He was soon gone. His empty coffee cup loomed as a remnant of his existence. Lila rinsed it and put it in the sink out of sight. She kept doing and redoing her makeup. Wishing it would cover more. She shrugged herself into a pink, lacy button-down blouse and blue jeans. Casual heels. She forced herself to eat a yogurt although she had no appetite. She brushed her teeth for the third time. She looked at her makeup and hair one more time. In the car, she felt her hands on the steering wheel shaking. "Oh God," she said out loud, "I'm too old to be doing this."

She had not considered the desk clerk. She froze. "two twelve" she blurted out. He simply nodded to her and she hurried past, feeling like a criminal. She took the stairs. She stood for a moment, pulling herself erect. It occurred to her that she may not like the way he looked. What then? She took a breath. Bernie crowded into her mind. She pushed him away. She rang the bell. And then the door opened.

Nothing was wrong with the way he looked. But it was unsettling not to see the young guy she had known all those years ago. His hair was grayer than it looked in pictures. He definitely still had lots of it. Cut a little longer than she would have liked. His dress was not as sophisticated as she had assumed it would be: A pair of cheap jeans, no-name sneakers, and a polo shirt probably from Target or Walmart. Not very different from his dress in college. His face was somewhat craggy and gaunt. That was the big difference, she realized. God, they had been so young. She focused on the eyes. She remembered them: intent, searching, dark brown. His shoulders were slightly stooped. He held a waste basket in his two hands. He held it out to her. "Need this?"

She frowned, not comprehending.

"Basin."

"Oh." She laughed. Then felt a wave of anxiety. "Do you?"

He shook his head. She walked in, glancing around the room. Not bad. Nice sized kitchen. A couch. A desk. And the king-sized bed.

He saw her looking at the bed. "It's very comfortable."

For a moment they stood gazing awkwardly at the bed. "So here we are," she finally said, turning to look him in the eyes. "I'm not the smooth-skinned, chubby butterball you knew."

He took her hand. His felt moist. He was nervous too. Good. "You're thin and fit," he said.

"I work out."

He led her to the couch, walked to the kitchen and brought back a bottle of wine and two glasses.

They sipped. Neither one of them knew quite what to say. Then he leaned forward and kissed her. That was abrupt, was her first thought. All she could think after that was, I have not kissed anyone but Bernie in four decades.

They drank wine. They talked. Soon the awkwardness began to dissipate. They were chatting as they did on the phone. Her head was resting on his shoulder. His arm was around her. He rose to fetch a second bottle of wine. They were kissing now more than talking, more than drinking. Clothing started to come off. The intensity of her feelings was now so high she finally jumped up. "Let's get into bed," she said.

She snatched the spread off the bed. Then she more carefully, methodically loosened the top sheet and blanket. She made sure to turn off the lights and close the curtains. In the twilight dark of the room, he removed her panties and his underpants. As they sank down onto the bed, she whispered in his ear, "I've been thinking about this all week; I can't wait."

"Me too. My heart has been pounding like I've been on uppers for days."

They spent the next five hours in bed.

"What are you doing?" he asked, lying against her, fondling her hair. He kissed her cheek.

"Texting Lorna and Lola. They have left me half a dozen texts, wanting to know I'm OK, that you're not an ax murderer." She was lying back on her pillow, holding her phone in the air, feeling a calm enveloping her. "And whether we did it." She typed, "OMG" and sent it off.

"What are you thinking?" he asked.

"I'm thinking that I cheated on my husband, after four decades."

He looked at her, but did not respond.

"And you know what? I don't feel guilty at all. I just don't. I want this. I deserve this." She rolled on top of him and slid him into her once again. "Oh God, I love having you inside me!"

As they lay together caressing each other she asked, "Do you feel guilty — at all?"

He thought about it. "I guess guilt is not the word. Worry. Worry for you. I have tried to point out things that could be risky. But as to guilt, I feel like if you are doing this, that is your decision."

"And I told you my decision. I want to be doing this." They kissed.

She grew silent.

"What are you thinking?"

"Just that Bernie trusts me."

On the last morning, she came to the hotel for a goodbye quickie. After they forced themselves out of bed and had coffee, she watched him pack. She took a picture of him in the room, their place. This ordinary hotel room would forever live in her memory as anything but ordinary. She walked out with him into the chill, dewy morning and waved goodbye. As she stood there, she was struck suddenly by the fact that her life was at a pivot point, and for the first time in as long as she could remember, she had no conception of her future.

Lila drove to the deli near her and got herself a bagel. Her friend Samantha was on the line. How odd it was to be having an ordinary chat about ordinary Harrisburg things on such an extraordinary day. Walking back to her car, she took in the scene: the bank where she knew the tellers, the gas station that always had the best prices, the coffee shop where she especially liked the strudel, the quieting post-rush-hour traffic she would drive home in. It was all so stable, so reassuring, and yet the pavement was cracking beneath her feet and every step she took now was uncertain, the turns unknown; her compass had lost its sure bearing. What should she do?

She knew this much; she had to make a longer next time happen. She sat on her deck formulating a plan. Her sister owned a house on the beach in Delaware. This year she was unable to get down there or rent it out. She had been after Lila to spend a week or two, make sure everything was in order. Lila had been putting her off. Anyway, Bernie couldn't get away. But, now, what could be more perfect? Alone together. No sneaking around. Complete privacy. Their fantasy world come to life.

⬥

It was a Friday night. Bernie was changing from his day-at-the-office clothes. He slid on a blue designer suit and was now knotting a yellow and blue striped tie. Lila turned from the mirror and he nodded with approval. "Stunning. You look stunning." He bent down and kissed her lightly on the lips so as not to muss her makeup. She had on a black, fitted dress, and pearls. She swept her hair back to reveal sapphire drop earrings. He glanced at his watch. "Ready?"

She nodded. "I'll just go pee pee," she said.

He was waiting in the Beamer. The restaurant was in Marysville across the river. An excellent steak house, it was set right on the Susquehanna at the base of the stone arch train bridge. She had wanted for years to get a picture of the bridge at sunset with a train coming across. For a few moments, the sun rays set the arches ablaze. Their grandson, Jerry, Diane's older son, loved trains and she wanted to give him the picture. But she had never managed to get the moment of sunset glow with a train.

"You have your phone ready for a picture?" Bernie asked.

"Yes, but I'm not hopeful."

"You'll get it one day. Maybe this is the lucky day."

They chatted about a legal matter he was up to his eyeballs in. Ages ago, Lila had worked at the firm as a paralegal when they were smaller and had hit a hard patch. She had wanted to pitch in. She had no formal training, but she picked it up fast enough with Bernie's tutelage. So she understood the lingo, and was interested in the story he was telling her.

After a while, they fell silent. She stared out the window at the trees and asphalt. Then, feeling desire overtake her, she picked up her phone and dialed Devin.

"Hi ya," he said. "What's going on?"

"I'm in the car."

"Where you headed?"

"We're going to a firm dinner at a great steak place."

"We?"

"Yup, that's it, Lola."

"Oh my God, are you insane? You think because you have the phone on your ear, he can't hear anything? Can't tell a male voice from a female?"

"What's that, Sweetie? The car is loud."

"I'm hanging up."

She put her phone down. "Lola had to go. Brad was shouting for her."

"How are they doing? We haven't seen them in quite a while. Has Brad fully recovered?"

"Yeah, he's fine. And you know Lola. Same old same old."

Bernie was hitting the gas pedal heavily. Lila sensed him giving her a quick look. "I'm a little taken aback when you call Lola by her real name. I have to think for a second who you're talking to."

Lila froze. After a moment she snuck a peek at Bernie.

They were crossing the river on the I-81 bridge. She could see the train bridge in the distance, the sun flaming the arches a fiery red. Three black engines led a freight train slowly west. "Well, no picture tonight," she ventured. "By the time we get there, it will be too late."

She glanced at him again.

"Next time," he said, smiling.

She let out her breath.

------◆------

A week after the illicit rendezvous, as she liked to think of it, Lila lay in bed reading some of their history of texts and emails, which had gotten racier and racier. Her mind and her body were still, after seven days, at an edge of excitement. But she realized these texts and emails were not something that should exist. As much as she didn't want to, she spent the afternoon with a nice white wine, deleting. Even that picture from the hotel had to go. When Devin called, she told him what she was doing.

"Good idea," he said.

"I don't think we are normal," she said. "At our age... All I think about now all day long is your cock."

"Not my pretty face? As I said, unresolved..."

"Yeah, yeah. Not unresolved now." She gazed out the window. The trees swayed gently in the bright sun. "We can't go on like this, you know, waiting for weeks and months between. Neither of us can stand it. I've been thinking about things. If we, if I left Bernie..." She paused.

He did not say anything at first. She felt a moment of panic she tried to calm. "I'm jumping the gun," she said.

"I guess we're both really serious, aren't we?" he said, his voice a little awed.

------◆------

Another glorious early June day. Sunny, breezy. Warm. Bernie was in his study working. Lila was on her computer trying to figure out little details of the July trip. She needed to speak with

Devin. It would be much simpler than texting. Trixie was asleep in Bernie's study. Lila felt too excited to take the time to get her. She put on her shoes and quietly walked out of the house, to the street, and headed down the sidewalk with her phone to her ear. She was trying to be more careful now, not just assume Bernie wouldn't hear if he were in another room. Nodded to old Mr. Schenker limping along with his bulldog. She returned to the house ecstatic. The date was set.

"Ca se passe, girls. July 12 we go. *Je ne peux pas croire.* Oh My God."

"Maybe we'll come down. What do you say, Doone? Kind of casually bump into you guys on the boardwalk."

"No fucking way."

They laughed.

Lila lay in bed reading over the last exchange of Delaware emails. She would need to delete them too in the morning. It was so exciting. They would be alone in a private world for two weeks. No worries about going out to eat. No sneaking around. She wished she had not deleted the past emails and texts; she really wanted to read over the dirty ones. She lay on her pillow drifting off to sleep, smiling. Her I-Pad dropped out of her hands onto her lap. She dozed.

"WHO IS DEVIN?"

She jerked awake. Still groggy, she looked up at Bernie, standing over her, his fists clenched. A chill shivered through her.

"Who is Devin Remson? Who?"

His shaved head was red. He was standing in a wrinkled, blue tennis shirt and briefs.

"What?"

"Devin."

"No one."

"No one? Who is Devin?"

She could not think of anything to say.

"I'll show you who he is," Bernie said, with a sadness in his shaky voice. He bent down and reached for the I-Pad. As she snatched it and pulled it back, he lost his balance and toppled onto the bed on top of her.

"Ow, my breasts," she cried. She tried to push him off. As they tussled over the I-Pad, they rolled over with their arms entangled, and both tumbled onto the floor with a thud. She felt blood on her lip where the I-Pad had banged into her.

He was crying now. Bernie was lying on the floor crying. "You're going to Delaware with this person? Who is this, this Devin that you are planning a trip to Delaware with?"

She pulled herself back up onto the bed, dabbed her lip with a tissue. Pulled the blanket tight around her. Bernie sat rigid on the edge, his eyes glittering lasers boring into her and then scanning her surface. Mapping her face, as if encountering it for the first time in a long while.

"He was a friend of mine in college," she started carefully. "I told you about him at the time. He emailed me recently and we have been corresponding on line. It's nothing."

"Nothing?"

She looked away as his eyes drilled into her. All she could think of was the last text she had deleted two days before. Thank God. "I'm going to sit on your mouth and you are going to lick and suck me till I come. Just like we did at the hotel."

"He lives not that far from my sister. We thought we might have lunch one day."

"He lives in North Carolina."

She felt her body sag; she could no longer control her muscles. She was weightless.

"I felt very guilty for looking on your phone," he said. "Very guilty. *I* felt guilty." He let out a bitter laugh.

She forced words out of her mouth. "It was a fantasy world. Not real. Nothing has happened. You have three loves: tennis, the law firm, and I am the distant number three." She shrugged.

He started to cry again. "I can't tell you how it hurt me to see you write that the two of you are soulmates. This person Devin Remson and you are soulmates." He sat sobbing. Then he walked out of the room.

Lila picked up her phone and called Lorna. "He found out."

"Lila, what happened?"

"I can't talk. It is really bad though."

"Are you OK? Are you safe? I can come over now with Jim."

"No, don't. Really. I'll be OK."

"If you have any doubts, whatever time it is, get in the car and drive over here. Keep your keys near you, I'm serious. On your person."

"Oh stop it. Bernie? Bernie would never hurt me. Stop being over-dramatic."

Expressing that truth to Lorna helped Lila put things in perspective. But she realized she was shaking. What had she done to her life? Oh God, what had she done?

⸻◦❖◦⸻

Bernie did not return to the bedroom and she did not leave it. She did not lock the door. She did not deserve to protect herself even if she thought she needed to, which she did not. In the morning, the sun that streamed into the bedroom seemed incongruous.

"Please don't email me or call today," she wrote to Devin. Then she added, "I'm sure you can guess what's going on."

After several hours she ventured downstairs, wrapped in a red linen bathrobe, her hair unbrushed. Bernie was sitting on the couch, staring into space. He had showered and dressed. That was a good sign. "I made some pancakes," he said. "I'm keeping them warm. Would you like some?"

"I would. Thank you," she said. She felt tears running down her cheeks. "I'm so sorry," she said.

"I love you," he said. "You said it yourself. I have three loves. I just got the order reversed. You are my whole life. I would be completely lost without you."

"I know," she whispered. "I am so so sorry."

"You are soulmates," he said, and started sobbing.

She could not think of anything to say.

"What horrifies me, what makes me want to cry out and scream, is how foolhardy, how dangerous this trip would have been. The risk you were taking. You have not seen this person in forty years. You know nothing about him. The thought of you alone in that isolated house in Delaware. Totally unprotected from this stranger. Anything could have happened. He could be a psycho. A rapist. You have talked to him on the phone a little. What do you really know about him? I can't bear to think about it. I am beside myself. What came over you?"

She did not respond.

"This was a thunderbolt. I have been thinking all night. I want to make everything up to you. I have taken you for granted. Everything you do so perfectly. I have neglected you. Do you want me to retire?"

"No, of course not."

A pained expression she could not bear to see came over his face. "Are you going to leave me?"

She opened her mouth, but no words came out. She sat staring at him. Oh God help me, please, she thought. To Bernie she said, "I am in a daze. I just can't think right now. I would like to go for a drive, just be by myself. Is that OK?"

"Of course."

She drove. She got onto I-83 and just kept going. She did not call anyone. She did not think about what to do next. She just drove, trying to calm herself with the motion of the car. She drove for three hours or so. She blasted music. She stopped at a rest stop for a hamburger. She watched the people coming and going, the world indifferent to her calamity. How cliched, she thought. And smiled. Then she turned around and drove home. To her home. To her home now. Her home, she said to herself over and over as she walked into the house.

⸻◆⸻

On Monday Bernie went to work late. When she was sure he was gone, Lila dialed Devin.

"He found out?"

"I'm sorry. Please don't be angry with me."

"I'm not angry. I feel awful for you. What happened?"

She told him. "We have been talking all weekend. He has been so good about it. Really lucky he doesn't know about last week. I am so torn. I love you. I love him too, and I've put over forty years into this marriage. Can I let it go now, can I? Give up my whole world. At my age. I'm so scared. And yet I want to be with you."

Devin was silent, waiting for her to go on.

"We resolved the unresolved sexual tension, I guess you could say."

"We did," he said. "And we got to know each other again."

"Yes, we did."

"Look, you've been knocked off balance. I don't think you can know what is right for you to do today, this week. It's not a moment to make any decisions. You need to take your time. I'm not going anywhere. You know how to reach me. But for now..."

She nodded. "How are you so wise?"

She was crying. She whispered goodbye and put down her phone.

She let herself cry for a while. And then she called Lorna and Lola together.

"I was so stupid. He kept warning me to be careful." Her mouth was dry. "It's so hard. Lola, how did you do it?"

"Gets had decades of practice," Lorna said.

"Ha," Lola answered.

"Bernie said I was acting weird the last couple of weeks. Ticked off a list of things that were not like me. Just a lot of little things. Devin tried to tell me that no man is as clueless as I thought Bernie was."

She felt her eyes tearing. "He's so trusting. He loves me so much."

"Yes he does," Lorna said.

"What really made him go and look at my emails and texts –"

"How was he able to do that? I don't understand."

"We have the same password on our phones and everything."

"Oh my God. Darling, you have got to be kidding me."

Lila started to cry again.

"Leave her alone, Lola. Jesus."

But Lola could not hold back. "Lila, reckless doesn't even begin to describe it. Maybe," she started to say and then stopped.

"You think I wanted him to find out?"

"I didn't say that."

"Maybe it's true. I'm so stupid."

"No," Lorna said.

"He never looked before."

Lola snorted.

"What finally told him something was going on for sure was the other day when we were planning the Delaware trip, and I wanted to talk to Devin while Bernie was home. Too complicated to text about it, and I couldn't put it off. I went out walking down the street so I could call him without Bernie hearing. I was proud of myself. I thought I was following Devin's advice to be really careful about him hearing. The thing is, I went without Trixie."

"Yeah? Go on."

"That's it. I don't ever go walking down the street talking on the phone without the dog. I would never do that. Why would I? It's not like I was out for a run. I just walked down the street and back. And he stood in the window of his study watching me. Alarm bells went off. Just a stupid, thoughtless mistake on my part. And then he looked at my emails."

"Oh God, what a cluster fuck."

"So now what do I do? I need help, girls. Am I being fair to Bernie not telling him that I actually slept with Devin. Do I owe him that truth?"

"Ouch," Lola screamed into the phone.

"I don't think hara-kiri is required," Lorna responded to Lila's question in a barely audible voice.

"Consider yourself lucky. You still have choices. Don't push it."

They talked for two hours, or maybe it was three. To Lila it had the dreamy feel of being back in the dorm on one of those many occasions when boyfriend trouble had become boyfriend disaster. She was sensing the twin beds, the posters on the walls, the stuffed animals. The ever-present commotion in the hallway as they talked. The conversations monotonously similar, but always new and urgent and so intense. And here they were again, all these years later, the three of them, the L-sketeers. Their bond made her feel that she could find her way through this and come out the other side ready to embrace whatever decision she made, whatever the future held.

The Country House

I SEE US AS in a snapshot: small distant figures in the wide sweep of hilly mowed lawn that stretched to the line below, behind the camera, where the grass was allowed to grow tall and wild. The fir trees beyond the tall grass hid the creek where we swam, with old black inner tubes encircling us, and fished from the wooden dock; sat with our legs dangling from the bridge that crossed the creek, the bridge that led nowhere but into a thicket of poison sumac trees; learned to row in the battered rowboat that summer after summer was wedged up in the mud and the slick weed clumps below the bridge, waiting for us.

I see us sitting in the stately red oak chairs with their white wooden wheels as tall as the chair arms themselves. We held high ball tumblers filled with iced tea or lemonade. In each tumbler stood a brightly-colored swizzle stick with a head shaped into an exotic jungle animal. I particularly insisted on a swizzle stick when Faith forgot. My aunt clomped up the porch steps, called into the cool darkness, "Faith, my nephew must have a swizzle stick with his lemonade. You know which one."

"I sure do," came the reply. And soon Faith appeared, round and soft, smiling warmly at me, extended hand offering the little stick with the hippopotamus head. Embarrassed to have brought her out from her kitchen, I peered down at the ground as she mussed my crew-cut head. She told my father how adorable I was, and how I'd grown.

I see this scene. I also hear it and smell it. The insistent rustling of the trees in the woods behind and on the sides of the house at the top of the lawn permeated every moment. The piney scent; the whiff of roses carrying on the breeze from my aunt's garden. The scent of my uncle's cigar in the summer air placed its lasting imprimatur on the country. Even now, just thinking of the lawn and the chairs and the lemonade, and the stone house, so cool inside, and the wooden porch with its special creaking sound, I smell the faint, delicious aroma of cigar smoke. The trace of cigar smoke on a blustery winter day, on a busy city street returns me years and miles to this summer place.

These summers that are otherwise timeless in my recollection marched onward in the images I see of my aunt doing her annual battle with the gnats. A handkerchief wrapped unceremoniously about her head, she stood among us, who talked and gestured around and through her machinations. I see her intently pumping her Esso flit gun of DDT; I hear that click click sound as she pushed the handle in and pulled it out, spewing forth acrid mist. A frown pinched her face, as she scoured the air for gnats to exterminate.

In later images, the woods, the house, the line of cut grass were unchanged, but stink pots were set about us, with oily smoke rising from them. Still later, when some older faces were no longer in the scene, and new faces appeared, new lovers, husbands, little children, my aunt stood among us, handkerchief around her forehead, spraying from an aerosol can.

Toward the end, the very end, when the stately wooden chairs, or the only remaining one of them, was on its side behind the tool shed, replaced by aluminum frame chairs of woven plastic bands that had already become old and frayed; when I was growing old enough to see my relatives as strangers full of exposed failings; when, in short, the magic had faded and I, even as I sat there with them, feeling superior, was trying already to recreate it, to reinvest the scene I was a part of with its past, lost magic; then came the electric bug zapper. As we sat, the words that now seemed mindless to the full-of-himself college student wafted over me as the insects fried. The battle my aunt fought single-handedly was never won, of course.

When my aunt died earlier this week, little stir was created. She had been in a nursing home far away in Florida for six or seven years, degenerating slowly, pretty much without her faculties at the end. She had faded from our consciousnesses as we from her clouded memory. Great-nieces and nephews and cousins had been born and had grown to adolescence who did not know her. Her death was only a formality. And a lifting of her daughter June's burden.

My aunt's funeral is on a rainy day. My boss looks at me with annoyance when I tell him I have to take the day off for a funeral. "The whole day?" he says. I stand my ground. If I do not go to the cemetery, I will have half a day to myself. "*Try* to make the three o'clock meeting," he says, turning his back on me.

We are stepping around puddles on the broken sidewalk in front of the funeral parlor. Inside, in the hushed, carpeted reception room, acquaintances are approaching June, my aunt's only living child, with that cautious, tentative step of people expressing a grief they don't really feel. June has gotten even heavier since I saw her at her brother Robby's funeral, a funeral that came unsettlingly close upon her sister Janice's funeral. June wears a somber, earnest expression that seems purchased for the occasion. I kiss her lightly on the cheek she proffers mechanically. She squeezes my hand as we stand in that next awkward moment. Then the small, milling group of people is filing into the chapel and I, still holding June's leaden hand, am left alone with all that remains of my aunt's family. June. June's husband Laurence. Ralph, Janice's husband. And Janice's two ill-at-ease girls. I study the girls. They are in actuality young women now — past college age, although neither has gone to college. I have not seen them since they were five years old and moved to California when the first of Ralph's business ventures failed.

Before there were these girls, before there was Ralph, I awoke in my aunt's country house in the room that had been Robby's. From my earliest days, Robby's life had for me the lure of exotic adventure. The picture of him in his starched khaki uniform, leaning on a tank with his friend Herman, stood as a fixture on the piano in the living room of my aunt's country house. In that photo, ancient when I first encountered it, Robby wore his hair in a crew cut. After the war, he became a lawyer and lived in Greenwich Village and knew famous people whose names I had never heard. I knew by the reactions of others that these were exciting names. But what those names were I no longer recall.

A few tokens of his childhood days remained in the bedroom in the country house. Vivid in my memory is a sheathed knife that I found in a drawer and prized for many years. The day I found it, Robby happened to be there with a woman. They whispered that she was his secretary and only eighteen. But I was not yet old enough to understand their arched eyebrows and lowered voices. She became his wife shortly thereafter, the only wife he was to have, and was gone by the next summer. Robby, when I came down with the knife, took it from me with a look of awe on his face, handling it, examining it carefully as if it were a relic of some sacred past time. He smiled faintly, that smile of his that had a mocking cast to it, that was usually accompanied by a wry, or, as I came to realize as I grew older and found myself emulating it, obscene or derisive comment.

When he looked at me, he asked simply, "Would you like it?" I didn't answer. I was standing, looking up at him, my mouth open. "Go ahead; it's yours."

There was little my father, sitting in a chair on the porch, tight-lipped, could do. I realize only in thinking back on it now that the rise Robby would get from his gift was its occasion. "Robby, do you think —?" his mother, my aunt, began anxiously.

"Mother." The bitterness in Robby's voice I hear now. Then, it was masked by the turn of the lips, the crinkled jowls, and the laughing eyes that looked to us all to join Robby in his amusement with his mother's silly anxiety.

My father was silent. He resisted real confrontation. I was told by my father afterward that I could touch the knife only when an adult was present.

I slept in that room because it was the one with the twin bed. It had always been my room on our weekends there. I bounced up early. The sun turned the air a fiery swirl of dust and the wall a shiny yellow. I tiptoed out into the silent hallway, into that dank country-house odor exaggerated by the emptiness and stillness of the dark corridors. I hurried past the room where my father slept, and the big master bedroom with its own bathroom, where my aunt and uncle would sleep till later than anyone I knew ever slept. I came quietly down the stairs, hearing the loud ticking of ancient clocks, and pushed open the squeaky screen door.

I could taste that first breath of country morning air. My bare feet were wet from the dewy grass. I hid behind the old shed that housed the lawnmower. Hoped to spy a deer.

A wizened hired man came and rode that mower — once I saw him, in a big straw hat, and with a cigarette hanging out of his mouth. In the earliest years I liked to sit on the mower, turning the steering wheel endlessly back and forth while my father, who must have been infinitely bored, stood patiently waiting.

My father was a very earnest man, unlike Robby. On one very hot night, we all sat on the porch watching the ballet of fireflies. My aunt was fanning herself and me with a paper fan. My uncle was sucking and chewing his after-dinner cigar, leaning back in his chair, and occasionally picking his teeth with the rolled-up cellophane wrapper from the cigar.

My father and Robby were talking politics. Their voices reached higher and higher decibel plateaus with each outburst of the cuckoo clock heard through the window. Goldwater this, Goldwater that. We moved inside when the sound of hands slapping mosquito-bitten thighs grew regular and the air grew chilly. The wood neatly stacked in the fireplace was set ablaze, crackling and hissing. The argument raged on. June's husband and Robby outnumbered and so out-screamed my disconcerted father. The heresy of being for Barry Goldwater was so in-conceivable to my father that he was goaded into the kind of shouting match in which I had never seen him engage.

At breakfast the next morning, the clicking of spoons in bowls of cereal was unaccompanied by other sounds. But the next summer, it somehow came out that Robby shared my father's view. He was reminded, heatedly, of his allegiance of that fero-cious July night the year before. "It must have been a dull party," he said, his mouth narrowing, his face breaking into a crinkly smile. "Needed a little livening up." My father's lips pressed tight then, and he said nothing for many minutes.

My uncle always said he would take me for a ride on the mower when I was just a year older. Next year seemed so close, so almost palpable. When my whole youth had been spent and my desire, I had never ridden the mower.

My aunt and uncle had always imagined the country house as the center of family activity. But June and Janice, both married, bought their own country houses, and were rarely with my aunt on the several weekends each summer when my father and I were invited up. No one knew where Robby was. I was always hungry for information on the subject. In France, running some sort of studio, we were told once, but it was all vague. Robby had stopped practicing law almost as soon as he became really successful. He broke my aunt's heart. "Re-dick-ill-us," she would say to me when I asked about him. He was her inevitable subject as I watched her make the icing for a chocolate cake. "Don't you think it is quite re-dick-ill-us? You wouldn't give up your profession and go traipsing around the world, all over the place at the age of forty, would you?" She was sprinkling a teaspoonful of coffee into the creamy ripples of chocolate. I loved her coffee icing. She made it especially for me.

She told me again the story of Robby's frenzied studying for the bar with his friend Herman. It was right before the war. "Night after night, they asked each other questions. Back and forth they went, back and forth. I brought them coffee. I told them they needed to get sleep. But still they stayed up and studied and studied. Questions answers questions answers. Books and books and more books."

One late Fall day on a ride to view the turning of the leaves with a woman I thought, as I sometimes do in the early days, perhaps I might love and marry, I realized we were not twenty minutes from the old place. On a whim, we drove by. The people who had bought the other house on the property — originally owned by old friends of my aunt and uncle when they were all young and in the first flush of being well-to-do — had built a swimming pool. So at the dammed-up creek that had been our swimming hole, the old dock was falling apart. The bridge across the creek was too far gone to step on. I stared for a while over the rickety boards at the sumac trees still swaying in the breeze as if no time had passed, still holding erect the dazzling red cones of poison I had been so sternly warned off. The old rowboat was no longer shoved up on the bank, but a couple of the black dirty inner tubes that had encircled us thirty years before, when we could barely fit our little arms around them, still lay in the weeds, partially visible, deflated.

◆◇◆

The rabbi looks and speaks like Averell Harriman in his last years. I wonder where June found him. The rabbi from my aunt's and uncle's synagogue in Brooklyn is long dead. The congregation, all its living members, have long ago moved to Long Island. "To be closer to Beth David," my aunt had once said, referring to the cemetery, in one of the only humorous thoughts ever to occur to her.

When you haven't been to temple in as long as June hasn't — in as long as I haven't, for that matter — where do you find a rabbi?

My aunt was active in Hadassah, in all the Jewish charities. Treasurer of this. Secretary of that. She was always to be found in a swirl of friends and organizations. Most of her friends are dead now. The organizations function without her. The funeral parlor is quite empty.

When my uncle died of a heart attack twenty-four years ago, we were in the same funeral parlor, many people crowded together. My aunt was inconsolably, violently wrenched with sobs. June and Janice, in their early thirties and late twenties respectively, were weeping in handkerchiefs. Robby was there, I am sure, but I can not recall him now. I have no picture in my mind of him in that scene.

For my aunt, as I turn from my pew to survey the sparsely filled rows, I count fourteen individuals scattered about. Not many relatives have troubled to take off time from work this dreary wet day. Her old maid, Faith, whom I thought had died years ago, is sitting in the sixth row by herself. It is more than a moment before I realize who she is, the years have so swollen and shrunken her once roly-poly body. She was, in my memory of those years in the country house, a sweet woman whose face lit up when she saw me year after year. "How you've grown, dear. How he's grown," was her greeting. I remember hearing something about a daughter who was a plague to her. But I never saw the daughter.

I am pleased when I see my father. We hug. I had meant to call him beforehand, but there never seems to be a moment.

What I notice, as I sit in the pew at the funeral home, is that the seam in the carpeted podium has come undone. The podium itself buckles as Averell sways. There is about the place, along with the solemnity that blows through the air ducts, a hurriedness of construction that mimics this hurried stop on the way to rest eternal. Old Averell, who has never met my aunt, croaks on. He understands that Mrs. Birmingham, one of the oldest and dearest friends of the deceased, would like to come up and say a few words. We all sit waiting. I do not know my aunt's friends. That she existed in spheres outside being my aunt I can not readily conceive. My eyes drift to the coffin, which is an elegant, gleaming mahogany, and looms around my shrunken, exposed aunt.

"Mrs. Birmingham," the old rabbi urges the stilled company a second time.

It was a strange twist of fate that Janice and Robby, in their forties and fifties, would die within six months of each other, while their mother, somewhere in her eighties went on living. She understood that Janice had died. But her mind was degenerating so fast at that point that she was fated to suffer the moment of tragic loss of her youngest daughter over and over, like a Sisyphusian punishment, for as long as she lived. Each day, she called out from her bed for Janice, and became testy at her daughter's tardiness, the wronged mother of an uncaring child. Robby, for as long as I can recall, had suffered under a similar accusation. His revenge was to be an uncaring son, only perhaps more subtle in his hurtfulness at fifty than he had been at fifteen.

Averell is nodding and nodding toward a portly woman with dyed red hair who gazes back blankly. "Mrs. Birmingham, please," he says, urgently now.

"MONTGOMERY?" An urgent question from a pew.

"MONTGOMERY!" An angry, disgusted shout from another pew.

Hearing her name, the portly woman starts.

And in a flurry of nodding and dipping his palsied head, Averell mumbles "Montgomery, so sorry, please madam."

Aflutter, the portly woman waddles to the podium. Mrs. Selma. Mrs. Mussel Shoals. It's all the same. Speaks of organizations, charities, Hadassah.

━━━◄O►━━━

Robby lost all interest in his relatives years ago. He did not appear at my wedding. Just as well, considering the duration of the marriage. Nevertheless, his mother was very upset with him about that. But, then, as we said to each other at the time, perhaps that was why he did not attend.

I doubt my aunt knew that Robby died before her. She was told, but who can say whether she understood. His death came six months closer to the end than Janice's death.

Robby died at the country house. It was decaying, and he had gone up to do some work on it. My aunt, it was by then clear, would never spend time there again. She spoke of it as it was in 1943, the year of sweltering July days when the water in the creek almost dried up and Robby spent the last hours with his friend Herman, the child of the other family on the property, before they both went to invade France. It was the last time Herman saw what that next somber summer would be named Herman Hills. At the time, no doubt, this memorialization of the property was done with the great dignity and entire solemnity aroused by the untimely, violent death of a son. To me, of course, he was not even a memory. The place had just always been Herman Hills, a name that meant summer. But when I arrived with that young woman, that autumn day, and she saw the name plaque at the entrance, her hysterical laughter did not stop ringing through the trees until we crunched up the winding gravel drive all the way to the house. "How could someone name such an exquisitely beautiful place *Herman* Hills?" she cried when she could catch her breath.

Robby, with power-of-attorney over my aunt's affairs, and with June's concurrence, and no sentimentality, was planning to sell my aunt's half share in Herman Hills. It had only bad memories. And a hundred wooded acres in this area were now worth a fortune. Staying at the house, doing some cosmetic repairs, he dropped dead of a heart attack.

We are three cars: the limousine carrying June and Laurence and Ralph and the two girls, my father's car with two aunts and an old uncle, and my car. We are idling on the side street, awaiting the hearse, and waiting for additional mourners to join the forming procession. So far none have.

The monotonous drizzle paints a rainbow on an oily patch of asphalt out my droplet-covered window. My eye follows an old black woman walking stiff-legged down the sidewalk across from me. She is attempting to open an umbrella that has gotten the best of her. I only recognize her as Faith in her shapeless raincoat and plastic rain hat when her face turns toward me as the umbrella bursts suddenly open. On an impulse I call to her. "Faith," I say. My voice is nearly drowned in the sooty wake of a passing bus. But she hears, turns slowly around, finally finds me, and walks with hesitant steps toward my car.

I feel robbed when she says "Yes dear?" with a tired sadness so unlike the vibrant jolliness I remember.

"Wouldn't you like to come to the cemetery?"

"Oh, no dear, that's OK."

"It's no trouble. If you'd like to come, it's no trouble at all."

"Well, you know, I would like to, thank you darling. I would like to. Yes I would. That's very sweet of you to offer. You always were a sweet boy." And for just an instant I see a hint of that smile I remember, and I find myself once more smelling the trace of cigar smoke in a country breeze and hearing the rustle of the fir trees in a clear blue sky.

The cemetery has many narrow lanes, puddled and indistinguishable, through the seemingly endless green fields of landscaped marble. Our procession, though, finds its way surely from lane to lane. My eye occasionally catches a name or phrase, "Bessie," "Beloved Father," "Let the soul go free," "She was a light by which all did see," "Our paths will cross again."

When we approach the grave site, the rain has ended, at least for the moment, but the overcast is heavy, the sky dark, the air misty. I spot Averell's head through the string of mourners slowly walking toward the grave.

Behind Averell, the grave diggers stand about in green, hooded slickers and mud-caked work shoes. They remind me of something from a Shakespearean comedy, six earth sprites, green creatures from below. Closer up, they are middle-aged men, except for one who is young and wears sunglasses. His hood is down and his blond hanging hair shakes wildly as he shovels dirt that has slid from the mound beside the grave. He flings it up the pile with quick ferocious strokes, while the others stand about watching us gather.

The coffin, resting on canvas straps, is lowered even before all of us reach the grave site. It slides and bumps its way into the gash in the earth, and Averell begins his praying. We are disturbed by the sprites, suddenly active again, climbing and crawling about the mound of clayish earth, leaning into the muddy hole, pulling and yanking at one of the straps, which has apparently gotten itself stuck under the coffin. They bounce my aunt, yanking at the weighty coffin at the bottom of the hole, disturbing Averell's speech to us about this good woman. They all pull together with grunts of effort, and the strap comes loose with a snap. Averell's weak voice fills the gray day. The now still gravediggers hover, one leaning against our family headstone, another sitting on the dirt pile, and others standing against adjoining headstones. The young one flings his shovel into the dirt pile. They watch our ceremony and wait.

We repeat after Averell, Yiska dal va yiska dash sh may ra bau...

Averill takes a shovel and touches it to the pile of dirt, flicks the grains into the hole. Then again, and once again. It sounds like rain drumming on a wooden porch. My Aunt Melody takes the shovel and fills it full of dirt. The dirt falls with a thud. She does this twice more. Then comes June, real tears at last starting to flow down her pudgy cheeks. Slowly, her entire plump body begins to shake. Her husband follows her, solemnly.

Averell, with outstretched hand, urges others. Looks at the girls. The older one shudders, refuses; the two of them step backward as one.

I come forward. Up close, the hole looks very deep. Against the shovel-marked clay walls, the jaggedly chopped roots of bushes a foot down shine moist and white. Below the roots, the four walls of earth descend to where the glossy coffin sits on the bottom, splattered with dirt. I pick up the shovel, fill it, and heave the damp earth down the hole. Then I refill the shovel, tilt it, and let the clumps of earth fall off the edge. I linger for a moment before I stick the shovel into the pile of dirt and step back.

"One more," Aunt Melody says sternly.

I pick up the shovel obediently and let the dirt slide down in a stream.

Averell says his last words and the mourners drift away.

The green men have moved in on their earth pile and are speedily filling the hole. I stand for a moment, watching as the earth closes about my aunt. The mound of dirt is quickly consumed. The young grave digger with the sunglasses scrapes a last bit from the ground, his shovel brushing against clumps of grass. He adds this dirt to the filled hole and pats the ground down with the back of his shovel. The other workers are already returning to their truck, talking idly. The young one rests on his shovel, smoking a cigarette, gazing off across the misty green field and the white stones.

I help Faith into my car, and we weave our way through the narrow lanes out of the cemetery. She is wiping the tears from her eyes. She is not exactly crying, but tears continue to run down her face as we ride in silence. "Your aunt was always so kind to me."

She subsides so abruptly that I find myself turning toward her. Her head is shaking back and forth as our eyes meet. "The first time my Jesse was in trouble, your aunt paid for me to have a lawyer. Lord, I just didn't know where to turn.

I say awkwardly, "I never really knew about your daughter."

"I'll never forget, your aunt, she just walked into the kitchen in those slippers she liked to shuffle around in when nobody but us was up in the country and an old yellow nightgown she favored. She stuck a check in my hand and the phone number of your uncle's lawyer, and she said that it was bonus money that I had earned and that the lawyer was expecting my call. I know your uncle gave her a lot of trouble about it. I heard them arguing."

Her words wash over me in a wave. It is as if the same dam that held back June's tears has broken in yet another place, releasing another flood from this long-still lake, this reservoir of pain.

We are riding on the highway back to the city now. I am not driving fast; I am driving quite slowly. The cars and trucks whush by us on the wet pavement, leaving a fine spray in their wake. The drab outskirts of the city to which we return blur against the gray, drizzly sky. The very sound of Faith's voice brings to my mind the hippopotamus swizzle stick in my lemonade, Faith handing me my glass on the country lawn. I want it back, all of it.

"It wasn't so easy in those days, raising a child by yourself," she says, too calmly, too reflectively. "She was a smart little thing. Quick as a whip. She was something." She is shaking her head slowly back and forth, smiling, then not smiling, sinking again. "I wish to the Lord I could know where I went wrong."

I want to share my memory of the lawn, the swizzle stick with Faith, as if it would give her solace too. But I am silent; I feel the country house receding — irretrievably — with every mile. Hands on the steering wheel, eyes ahead, I listen to Faith's voice, barely a murmur.

"She told me I cared more for my families than for her. She left me. She just disappeared. Oh it was a terrible time. Still now, when I think about the wide world, and she's somewhere —. You didn't know about any of this? Well, some things are better to let lie. Your daddy knew best not to tell you."

"My daddy," I start to say, and then don't know what I want to say. Maybe that I know how much he loves me.

"I was in the hospital two months. I broke down. Not having any insurance, I lost my apartment. Your aunt, of all my people that I worked for, she was good to me. She took me in. That's how I came to work for her full-time, live in. You probably don't even remember a time when I didn't live with your aunt, do you? Oh me. Oh my. Long time past. Long time ago."

The Slugger And Henry Joraleman

HENRY JORALEMAN AT FIFTY-ONE years old: within a newly-sprouted nose hair of a promotion that would catapult him across the divide between middle management and executive privilege; still with the face of a forty-five-year-old and all the hair on his head, but the first disturbing strands of gray commencing their encroachment; divorced two years from a wonderful woman, whose hair seemed still, in her absence, to find its way into his scrambled egg and inexplicably clog his bathroom sink. Henry Joraleman, sitting this summer day in his eight-by-eight office, gazing out the window.

Henry would have had an impressive view from his eighteenth-floor window if a big, black, glass box of a building directly across the street did not obstruct the vista. There it stood, affronting him daily, ugly in all seasons. In the winter, when darkness came early, the black glass dissolved at twilight into layer upon layer of men, and a few women, at desks, and Henry found himself growing infinitely depressed as he stared blankly through his window at these multiple images of himself. Once, looking upon these scenes of commerce, Henry was privy to a shocking drama enacted on a desktop in utter defiance of all those rules of corporate decorum handed down by the highest authorities and disseminated in a flurry of electronic-mail memos by his and every other human resources department. But today, in the steamy summer midday, the building loomed, its secrets well covered, a big, black eyesore reflecting the glaring sun.

Henry was in his post-lunch slump. His eyelids kept drooping closed, and the torture of holding them open made him dream of clamps, until that image was overwhelmed by the thought of the soft, comfortable sofa in his boss Tilly's office. Henry had tried everything to avoid this sluggishness: limiting lunch to a fruit salad — but then he ate a candy bar, more like two, by four o'clock; cottage cheese — after two days he couldn't fork it in without gagging. It didn't matter; any food eaten at the lunch hour put unbearable weight on his eyelids. So why bother with restraint? He had just had tuna salad slathered in mayonnaise on a buttered roll, a bag of potato chips, and a pint of chocolate milk. He jerked himself up from his chair and started out of his office to circulate his blood, deny that sticky cholesterol his ex-wife had fretted over for so long a chance to grab on to an artery wall.

"Look what I got." It was Roscoe, his comrade in rank, his main rival in the climb up the slippery, narrowing pyramid of the organization. Roscoe stood in the hallway with his barrel-shaped gym bag slung over his arm. Roscoe liked to spend his lunch hours at the gym. His platelets no doubt sailed unobstructed, singing merry tunes, through arteries clean as a whistle. Henry was too old for the gym; all those smelly bodies, other people's sweat on the machines, and say what you will, he didn't like showering in those open stalls with half the men in the city more interested in someone in the next stall than someone in the next locker room. Henry had owned an exercise machine, he'd even set it on "hill" every now and then under duress, but Doris took custody of the machine when she left. She didn't take much and he was not sorry to see the thing go.

Roscoe was beaming over a black and white photo, an eight by ten, of a baseball player that Henry instantly recognized as the great pitcher from his youth. It was an old fashioned posed photo. In it, the pitcher was bending forward, eyes riveted on the camera, legs spread wide, glove hand back, throwing arm forward, the static after-pose of a pitch that was never delivered. It was autographed in bold black marker.

"He's over at the new sports memorabilia store," Roscoe said offhandedly, unlocking the door of his office.

"Why didn't you tell me?" Henry said, feeling hurt.

"You're not a baseball fan."

In point of fact, Henry was not a baseball fan. He couldn't even tell you the names of all the new teams of the last thirty years or their leagues, much less divisions. He couldn't tell you who was on the team now. But in his youth, when there were no divisions, just two leagues with ten teams each, when the pitcher was playing, when his team was playing – some would say the greatest team that ever played, better than the Yankee machine of the days of Ruth and Gehrig (you could argue, but statistically it wasn't a contest) — then Henry was a fan. Back then, Henry raced home from junior high school every day to catch the end of the game. Usually he would get there some time in the fourth inning, see at least half the action.

"He's gone I guess now?"

Roscoe looked at his watch. "No, he'll be there for another ten minutes actually."

Henry disappeared into his office, swung his jacket on, and double-timed down the hall. Platelets clung to artery walls for dear life.

The line, which had, according to the guard, sprawled up and down aisles until well after two o'clock, was now, at 2:25, not long at all. Henry stood breathless, hiking up his pants and looking around him. A couple of teenagers wearing earrings and backwards baseball caps shopped for team jackets. One of them asked Henry who it was at the table, and when Henry told him, he said blankly, "Who he?"

Henry was dumbfounded. "Probably one of the ten best pitchers there ever were," he said. The kid shrugged with a slight discomfort.

"Yeah?" the kid said, and glanced at the little guy sitting at the table, bent over a glossy photo of his former self.

Was fame so narrow? Henry looked at the kid's unformed lumpy face and his sparkling earring, and confronted the horrifying thought that his whole store of accumulated information was time-bound, his lifetime of knowledge worth only a shrug of dismissal from this emissary of a future world. He felt suddenly dizzy, and leaned his weight on the corner of a shelf of sweatshirts.

"You OK?" the kid asked.

Henry Joraleman stood in this emporium of memories, suddenly, momentarily, terrified by the vision of a hairless, wrinkling, shrinking self, trudging forward, wifeless, solitary, into a dark, alien century.

"Yeah, I'm all right," he mumbled.

The line moved quickly forward until Henry was at its head. Standing now in front of the former rookie southpaw sensation, former wily old veteran, still young-looking old white-haired man, Henry tried to make him know the importance he held for Henry: "I spent many a day racing home from school to watch you pitch," he said. You all inhabited my being; you were more real to me than my junior high school life, he could have said.

The man was neatly – as methodically as he pitched – signing the picture, as requested, "To Henry," but he didn't respond to Henry's words. Didn't even make eye contact. He was already reaching for the next picture as he handed Henry his.

Not being able to connect left Henry with a certain empty feeling from the experience, but he pushed it away, didn't let it trouble him. The meeting was a little impersonal, Henry thought, but the man had been signing for two hours already. Henry was mostly happy to have the photo with the autograph. He bought a simple frame for the picture at the drug store and hung it on his office wall.

As one day drifted into the next in the sameness of train to the city and train home, as his droopy-eyed gaze fell at odd moments on that black-and-white reminder of years long gone, Henry began to realize that this autographed photo on his wall was not fully satisfying. It was calling out for another — for the autograph Henry had desired so desperately all through his childhood. The slugger! The slugger who had been his idol.

The acute awareness that the slugger — never a very healthy specimen — was aging even as Henry thought about him made the need to acquire that autograph feel urgent. Rather suddenly one day this urgency took control of Henry. He asked Roscoe if he thought the slugger would ever come to the sports memorabilia store. Roscoe shook his head. He doubted it. This had been a grand-opening event. He wouldn't expect them to have anyone again soon, much less someone as renowned as the slugger. So how would he find the slugger, Henry wondered. Roscoe said the slugger had signed a book for him a couple of years ago at a bookstore, his autobiography he had just written at the time. Now? Roscoe didn't really know. He had no idea. Henry could kick himself. Where had he been? Why wasn't he thinking of this a couple of years ago? He had read about the book coming out. He'd probably seen the ad. Why hadn't it seemed important then? Roscoe said that he wouldn't sign anything but the book then, but Henry thought he'd have agreed to a picture if Henry bought the book. Why not? But where to turn now?

It was Henry's boss, Tilly, who acquainted him with the demi-monde of baseball cards and autograph signings that sprang up on a Saturday morning only to evaporate away by sunset Sunday. "Check the ads on the Friday sports page," Tilly told him without much enthusiasm. He said the slugger did appear every once in a while. "You may have to travel a ways. You'll find him eventually if you keep looking. But you'll pay through the nose."

"Pay?" Henry was shocked. Pay for an autograph? He remembered those halcyon days at the stadium, that baked, heavy air, the scent of summer, as he stood outside the players' exit in the August twilight after nine innings of pyrotechnics, waiting with crumpled program and pen, hands shaking as a player rushed out in street clothes. A thrill as the face of a human being up close clicked as a famous black and white face from his TV set. Straining forward, thrusting his program up, taking it back, if he was lucky, with the magic name indelibly there, on his program, in his hand. He could not imagine this as a cash transaction. "That'll be $5.98 kid. $6.02 with tax. No, sorry I don't have change of a twenty. Out of ten. Do you have two cents?"

He had gotten maybe a third of the team, maybe it was closer to half, over his junior high years — he would have to go through his boxes of stuff and look — but he never did get the slugger. He got to know which players never signed. He tried everything he could think of. He tried bringing self-addressed postcards, gave one to the second baseman as he brushed by. He sent it back signed, postmarked from his hometown deep in the South. But the slugger always bulled his way through; couldn't give him anything. Once, though, he spied that familiar single digit on the license plate of a fancy car sitting at the curb waiting, and he strode boldly up to the window and slipped a card through to the blonde woman sitting in the front seat smoking a cigarette. She said she would have him sign it. "What's your name?" He pointed to the front of the card. "Oh, right." She laughed. She said she would have him make it 'to Henry.' How was that? "Great," he had said, sheepishly, averting his eyes from this woman, the slugger's woman. He waited for the mailman for the rest of the season before he gave up. What had his father said to him? The card was probably lost before he ever got it. The woman probably put it in her pocketbook and forgot about it. Henry nodded, but he didn't think that was true.

That was a long time ago. He could not recall looking at those old autographs in decades; was not sure he even still had them. His interest was certainly not in filling out a collection. He heard Doris's voice: "What are you trying to do, relive your childhood? One Friday afternoon, several weeks later, Henry stood at the lobby candy counter trying to make the difficult decision among too many tempting confections. He remembered it was Friday and flipped through the sports section of the newspaper just in case. Halfway down the column of announcements, there it was, that magical name, "Special Guest: Autographs $50." Fifty dollars! Plus five dollars admission.

Although he was taken aback by the price, Henry could not resist calling the number given in the paper for information. The man on the other end was very patient with his ignorance. He had no idea. He had thought he would just come over, buy a photo, get on line, and that was it. Not so. You needed a ticket. The great man would sign his name exactly seven hundred times and six hundred and fifty people had already received their tickets. This appearance had been announced in some obscure journal six months ago and all the tickets were gone one week later. Fifty tickets had been held back and would be available at the door, first come first served. Doors open at nine. "You should have a decent chance if you are there by eight," the man said.

Henry thought it all through. This was it, he knew. If he weren't going to do it now when it was in the city rather than some out-of-the-way suburb, he wouldn't do it at all. But fifty dollars? And his weekend, his Saturday morning, his day to sleep late! With only fifty tickets available he was not the kind of person who was going to take any chances. He was not the kind of person who had gotten where he was without being utterly anal. What's more, he didn't believe there would be fifty tickets. Nothing was free of corruption now. Everyone had a friend they would slip a ticket to, and by the time he was standing at the door maybe there would be twenty tickets. Maybe not even, how would he know? And what redress would he have if he came all that way and the tickets were gone in advance? He would have to be there by seven, maybe before seven. He looked at the train schedule. He would have to get the very first train at 5:10. He would have to get up at 4:30. As if to Doris, his ex-wife, he tried to justify doing this. He couldn't. But something kept telling him he would be unable to keep from regretting it if he didn't do it. It was only one morning's effort, after all, and he would meet the slugger, would own the signed picture forever.

———◆———

The morning mist was heavy at the train station. That unmistakable woodsy scent of summer dawn blew through the chilly air. The sky was lightening, but the sun was not yet visible. Henry Joraleman was alone on the platform this Saturday morning. He paced, and his steps echoed in the stillness. He could hear

Doris's voice, lush with incredulity at the ridiculousness of what he was doing, a grown man, and even with her gone he started to feel silly, and, unaccountably, guilty.

Right on schedule he saw the glow of light in the distance that would become his train. It slid through the curtain of mist into the new morning, nighttime-yellow light dripping from its windows. When the doors clattered open, he was startled to see the number of human forms strewn about the car in unsightly positions of slumber and mummified positions of morning shock. Where were these people going? He had a frightening intuition they were going where he was going. He saw a baseball cap on at least two guys. He began to worry that with the people from this train alone he would be past number fifty. With a great effort he forced reality in and calmed himself. It was a big city; lot of things to do at five a.m.

He drank the coffee he had packed and ate two chocolate glazed donuts. Since Doris left, he had been buying all kinds of things she had not permitted him to have. Look at all the effort she had put into controlling cholesterol levels in veins she would abandon before reaping the reward of her vigilance. Life was inefficient.

At ten minutes to seven, Henry stood before the church that was hosting the baseball card show. No lines poured out into the street.

Several vans and station wagons were pulled up to the curb and a bunch of moms and pops stood unloading cartons. Henry followed a wheezing man hugging an oversized crate into the church and up a flight of curving stairs.

He peeked into the high-ceilinged room. It was split by a sliding door, now open, into an empty area in the back, and a sanctuary with dark wooden pews in the front. The light of the new day broke through in the vibrant colors of stained glass windows above the pulpit. The back area was in process of assemblage. Tables going up, displays unfolding; boisterous talk and phlegmy laughter emanating from graying men in golf shirts and baggy jeans hauling cartons and emptying them onto table display cases. Cards, pictures, bats, balls, uniforms.

"Can I help you?" a woman asked him. She had a cigarette hanging out of her mouth, a weathered look about her.

"I wanted to get a ticket."

She looked at her watch. "Not for two hours."

"I thought there'd be a line," Henry said apologetically, feeling foolish, out of place. Wishing he hadn't done this.

She pointed to the curving stairs. "Set yourself on down."

"So there *are* still tickets?"

She cocked her head. "Sure are. Fifty tickets, nine o'clock. You'll be the first," she said, fixing a professional smile on him that revealed all her teeth and gums. Then someone called her and Henry was relieved to be forgotten; the idiot who arrived two hours early.

Henry wondered how the slugger would make his appearance, and when. It seemed so hard to believe that, after thirty years, in just a short while the paths of the little boy and the great star would intersect at this unlikely place. He wondered if the blonde in the car had lasted the course. What was the slugger's life like, and what did he make of all those events that were so long ago? Events in Henry's own life from ten or twenty years ago, much less thirty, hardly seemed a part of his existence. Except maybe those days at the stadium. Even now he remembered with a thrill one ninth inning with only days left in the season and the pennant on the line. The bases were loaded. The score was tied. As so often, it all came down to the slugger. He had a habit of walking a lot and striking out a lot.

One or the other would decide the game. He did not do either one. He smashed a monumental grand slam home run.

A long-haired man of forty in a tee-shirt, the kind of freak he would expect to see at a flying saucer convention, was attempting to set his corpulent body down behind Henry. The last few inches separating rear end from step were more than his aging knees could control and he crashed heavily down with a grunt. As the line grew, the rest of the crowd seemed normal enough, but Henry had expected to find kids, teenagers. Most everyone on line behind him was middle aged. His age!

The flying saucer nut was a friendly enough guy. From him Henry learned that arriving early would not shorten his day. Once they bought their admission and autograph tickets, they would line up for the autograph in order of ticket number, not arrival time. They would line up fifty at a time. When Henry finally held his ticket, it was indeed number six fifty-one. He would not even be allowed to begin standing on line until afternoon.

Henry began his day wandering the narrow, tightly-packed aisles of this house of cards that had materialized from a bare space before his eyes. He bumped and squeezed his way from dealer to dealer; viewed displays of cards, plaques, balls, bats, uniforms, and pictures of every size and description.

He had wanted to witness the arrival of the slugger, but he was deep in this Casbah when he heard the murmurs, and the next thing he knew, the announcement was made over the loudspeaker that those with tickets numbered one through fifty should line up in the front. Henry hurried as best he could to catch a first glimpse, but it took him a while to extricate himself from the maze.

At last he emerged and walked up the center aisle to the front of the sanctuary. There, up the steps, at a long folding table, sat the great man, beams of multicolored light streaming through the stained glass windows above his head. On display the slugger sat, a massive presence in a fancy white sweat suit, his powerful legs spread wide, his feet in white leather shoes planted firmly on the floor. Henry looked up at a face so familiar, older, but utterly the same as the one imprinted in his brain. He felt the same thrill he had felt as a child. The slugger paused to wipe his forehead with a cloth, and bent over a photo of himself.

On either side of him perched an official. The task of the man who sat on his right seemed to be to take the ticket and position the item for the slugger to sign. The woman on his left was charged with the task of handing him the appropriate implement from an arsenal of pens and markers. There were blue and black markers, white pens for dark surfaces, opaque ink and translucent ink, narrow tips for balls, wider tips for photos.

Henry watched for several minutes, and then he went back into the labyrinth in earnest to find the photo that would adorn his wall, that would be turned magical by the inscription to come. The first couple of hours passed quickly as he examined photos, keeping his ear cocked for the numbers being called out, finally choosing a black and white shot of the slugger blasting one of his tape measure jobs.

That accomplished, Henry walked to the sanctuary and sagged into a pew. "How you doing?" he said to the penitent sitting in the next pew, a respectable looking thirty-year-old wearing a baseball cap and sweatshirt, and keeping an eye on his little son crawling on the floor. The man nodded. He had in front of him a mounted photo at least six feet high by four feet wide of the slugger and the great Yankee of an earlier time, the two of them standing side by side, each holding a bat, smiling benevolently out on the world. The great star's signature in black marker ran across, above his knees.

The man saw Henry looking at it and said, "Nobody's gonna get anything like this again. He won't sign anything bigger than eight by ten."

"You're kidding?"

"Hasn't for a while now. I flew out to Chicago three years ago when I heard that was the last time he would sign anything bigger. With the both guys autographed, this'll be worth one, maybe two thousand."

"You're kidding?"

"At least. One of them dies, a lot more."

"But why won't he sign?"

He shrugged.

"He won't sign anything bigger than eight by ten?" Henry said, and couldn't help asking again, "Why?"

"Hey, he's the great one, he can do what he wants. What can I tell you?"

"But he's everybody's hero. You mean you come all the way to a show and you pay the admission and you pay him the fifty bucks or whatever he gets and you walk in with an eleven by fourteen and he won't sign it?"

"You got it. I've seen him refuse."

Henry pointed toward the slugger. "But he will?"

"Oh yeah, he doesn't care about the size."

"It's crazy," Henry said.

"Hey, the super-star from the seventies, who's name I refuse to speak, won't sign a bat unless it has another signature on it. I was doing a bat of the five hundred club — you know, all the guys who hit over five hundred home runs — and I brought him a clean bat, I was starting it with him, he happened to be the first, and he wouldn't sign it, told me, 'You get someone else on there first.' They don't want to create value for you. Some of them won't do bats at all, only pictures or balls."

"Bats are more valuable?" Henry asked, amazed at the intricacy of this arcane world.

The guy nodded, "Yeah, uniforms are the most valuable, bats are big. Balls less."

Pointing to the slugger, Henry asked, "He'll do clean bats?"

"Oh yeah, no problem."

Henry told him, "I don't want anything fancy, just a simple eight-by-ten photo signed 'to Henry' to put on my wall. I'm not interested in how much it's going to be worth. I just want it, you know?"

Henry showed him the picture.

"Nice shot."

"Black and white seems more authentic, don't you think?"

"Depends on what you want. By the way, he won't do personalizations."

"What?"

"He won't sign it to you."

"Why?"

"He just won't. Doesn't do it."

"But that would lessen the value if anything."

"I know, but he won't do it."

"Well, that doesn't make sense," Henry said, fighting his disappointment. "I'm gonna try," he said, confident the slugger would do that simple thing for him.

"Good luck."

"What number you got?"

"Four fifty-seven."

Henry sighed. "I got six fifty-one."

"Figure one o'clock, maybe later."

"Yeah."

After a while Henry wandered back to the front to watch. A man his own age with a belly a lot bigger than his, but also with a wife, a wife with a camera, handed a photo and a ball to the official, who handed them to the slugger, while the wife snapped a picture. Surely the slugger would sign the picture "To Henry." It would be so impersonal without that. He could have bought it in a store.

A man who was undoubtedly a dealer came bearing an attaché case filled with boxes of balls. Each box in its turn opened, balls removed and handed over. Each inscribed. The slugger signed them all. With each signature, he made the dealer money. Seven hundred tickets. Seven hundred signatures. The great man a commodity, happy at wholesale.

Finally they called for everyone with numbers over six hundred to line up. Henry, weary and hungry, his back aching, stood on line rehearsing the speech he had spent the last hour working up. He would tell him he had been waiting thirty years for this, that he had traveled all the way from – what seemed reasonable? Ohio? Virginia? Delaware seemed about right – Delaware and couldn't he just sign it to Henry? It would take a second. He wasn't a dealer. He just wanted it to hang on his wall. Or maybe that sounded too whiny. He would tell him he had waited thirty years and come from Delaware just for this. And smile winning-ly. Or he could say it was for his five-year-old son, named Henry. Silently, he recited these several speeches in various tones of voice as the line moved slowly on.

At last he was mounting the steps and handing his photo to the guardian beside the slugger. As the slugger took it, without looking up, Henry spoke. He heard his voice crackling out thin and weak. "Would you mind signing it 'To Henry?' he said, but the slugger had begun speaking to the woman who sat on his left. Henry recognized that familiar drawl. As the slugger started to sign his name, the woman was now responding, and Henry repeated his request a little louder, more urgently. "Could you sign it 'To Henry'?" The slugger looked up at Henry.

Nothing much moved on the craggy face, but the word came out unmistakably, coldly: "No." Enunciated cleanly, crisply, expertly; without drawl. The harshness of the voice vibrated from one hemisphere of Henry's brain to the other. There was a stubbornness, a petulance about it, a distant hint of an adolescent on a sandlot hunkering down.

Henry was taken aback. No longer the corporate executive, his imagined smiling speech that would win over the hero deserted him unspoken. Feeling a lightness in his stomach, he stuttered uncertainly, "You can't do that?" He felt humiliated, begging.

"No." The muscular shoulders and neck flexed. The gray eyes narrowed. There would be no explanation, no instant of camaraderie between longtime fan and hero, no kindly "I'd like to, but they won't let me," or "Sorry, but I have to stick to the ground rules or people would be waiting even longer," or even just "You know better than that," with a teasing smile.

Henry felt himself in a familiar place; he was in his kitchen, withdrawing, shrinking into himself as Doris lashed out in a sudden rage. Henry knew he should not push the slugger with another sentence, with his rehearsed speech. And he felt, with an intense clarity, his pitiful condition; he was a fifty-one-year-old corporate clone begging an over-the-hill jock to scratch his name on a picture of a moment gone thirty years, paying him a ludicrous amount of money and lacking the power even to negotiate for something so small and easy for the other to give as a scribbled five seconds worth of "To Henry." He was the aging mortal, confronting an ageless indifferent god. Henry picked up the picture and hurried off, until he was comfortably hidden in the milling throng. He could feel Doris shaking her head, saying, "What a mistake."

But several days later, on his lunch hour, Henry bought a frame to match the one in which he had encased the photo of the pitcher, and he hung it on the wall in his office. Over the months that followed, as people came into his office for various business reasons, their eyes were drawn directly to the photograph. They would walk over to the wall for a closer look. "That real?" they would ask, and Henry would nod proudly. And usually they would say, "Wow." And then Henry and the visitor would discuss the great player and recall various of his feats in reverence, and sometimes they would forget about their business.

Nicky And Cat: A Romance

E CATERINA IS FIVE FOOT even and Nicky is five eleven. Looking down at the top of her head, which rests against his ribs as they walk arm in arm, he smiles at the way her thin hair, clipped short and more or less freakish, but undyed natural brown — not green, not orange — juts out in all directions. Seen from the front, head on, her hair gives her a look that moves between shocked and worried.

It is their first time out together after having met one night the week before at a coffee shop on the Upper West Side of Manhattan where she goes to college and he lives. They had talked for hours that night. Maybe it was all that caffeine talking; maybe they really hit it off. They still didn't know the answer to that question when they started out today. Now they are thinking they do know. They are both pretty excited.

This is an afternoon date, made because neither of them wanted to wait until they both had a free evening. Nicky has tickets to the ballet with his friend Carla this evening. Ecaterina is going club hopping with her friends.

Her eyes are concentrating on their feet, his in blue running shoes, hers in white sandals. She is playing at keeping in stride with his longer legs. He notices, as he has more than once already, how gracefully she moves, how even walking in this awkward position, her control of her body is all but total. She has been daddy's little ballerina, she told him earlier, since she was ten.

This perfect late-May day has passed faster than they realized. They have no time for the Japanese restaurant they had planned. Now they are thinking about heading in their separate directions and she says she wants to stop and get cigarettes. He doesn't like the fact that she has been smoking — because she is young and he feels in a certain way protective of her (crazy as he knows that is on a first date), and also because he stopped smoking himself years before, but always lapses back when he is seeing a woman who smokes.

At a newsstand, she is pulling loose bills out of the back pocket of her stylish white linen pants.

"It's hazardous to your health," Nicky says without conviction.

She replies, as they begin walking again, "Actually not, at least in an immediate sense." She lights the cigarette with quick little moves, then shoves the pack in her back pocket.

He gives her a questioning look when she glances his way. She keeps walking, but responds by tossing off something about her blood sugar level dropping when she smokes.

"Is that good?" He laughs. "What, you measure it?"

Walking on, taking a puff, she replies, off in front of him, "Yah," with a quiet vehemence that says, "Obviously I do; of course I do." And then she says, "I'm diabetic."

"Oh," he says. And doesn't know what else to say.

They walk on, she putting her cigarette to her lips for an instant. She has a way of biting off a nip of smoke and then letting it drift out between her slightly-parted lips — the upper one so sexily full — in a long, lazy stream. She makes a cigarette look delicious.

"Cigarettes aren't good for diabetics," Nicky says with a frown. "Are you sure you should be doing this?"

"Look, I just wanted you to know," she offers. "Not have it come up later. It's just a part of who I am. Not a big deal."

Nicky smiles. "I'm getting ahead of myself, aren't I? I'm sorry." He is excited by her words: come up later.

She shakes off his apology. "I've had a really good time," she says as they part. He kisses her lightly on the lips.

———— ❈ ————

Nicky is hurtling down Broadway in a taxicab. At Lincoln Center he lopes up to the Met, where a rumbling Carla stares at her watch at three minutes to eight. "This is inexcusable. This is the last time I'm holding your ticket. Do you hear me?" She wheels and lumbers off, and he hurries after her.

"I'm in heaven," he says in answer to her demanding glare when they are settled in their seats.

"Another blonde thing; why else would you be late? I should have known it."

After the ballet, Carla and Nicky are sitting at a small round table, one of the row that runs the length of the narrow bar at their habitual haunt, a dim-lit tavern, beery and thick with smoke. They are at the table nearest to Elsa's piano, which is in the back, against the smoky-mirrored wall, and surrounded on three sides by what has always looked to Nicky like long slabs of black kitchen counter. A dozen or so stools are lined up around the counter. Behind the stools, a cramped space of floor is always filled with crowds of standing "Music Lovers" as Elsa calls them when they whoop over the red hot songs. Right now, though, it is cool blues, and mellow with "Stella By Starlight" just concluding.

"Well?" Carla demands, "Let's have the whole sordid tale. Where did you find this one?"

Nicky smiles. "I barely know her, but it feels so right."

Carla snorts. "My, my, do I hear the familiar strains of an old tune? Have we another stranger-goddess here? An emotional cripple, no doubt. Any slash marks? Did you check her wrists? I shan't pick you up again. I'm tired of it. Do try to realize — now — that she's earth-made, earthbound, just a human being. So you won't be quite so startled later, when you actually know her." Carla shows him teeth and wiggles her eyebrows.

"Stop it," Carla scolds him. Nicky is lighting a cigarette he took from Ecaterina's pack. Carla jerks it away from him and crushes it out.

Elsa's satin-smooth voice fills their silence. Billy, the waiter, sets down Nicky's beer and Carla's gin and tonic. Carla arranges hers in the center of her napkin.

"Run a tab, Billy," Carla says.

Elsa's voice floats over them, singing about Miss Otis, and what she regrets.

Nicky pours his beer into the glass. Carla is stripping her lime slice from its peel with her teeth. It comes away cleanly.

"So what's the blonde thing's name?" Carla asks, chewing.

"She isn't blonde. Ecaterina."

"Eyy-kat-tereeeeena?" Carla repeats.

"Ecaterina," he echos, liltingly.

"Oh, shut up," Carla says. "What's wrong with her?"

"What?" Nicky takes on a truculent look as he stares back at her.

Elsa, at the piano, is going hot now. Nicky cannot remember if the bit of domesticity she is describing is performed by her "Handy Man" or her "Kitchen Man." The dozen or so people standing around the piano don't ponder, but come to life with raucous approval. "Whew!" "Go Elsa."

Carla will not, however, be diverted. "Wrong, what is wrong with her?"

Nicky relents, with a sheepish look. "She's just a tad young, is all," he says.

"Tad, tad, what are we talking, thirty, twenty-eight, twenty-five, twenty-two?"

"A tad more."

"Twenty-three? Twenty-four?"

"No, a tad more young."

Carla groans. "Idiot. Is she even twenty?"

"I'm not sure. Maybe just. Nineteen or twenty."

"What could you possibly have in common with her? Yes. I know, I know, don't — even — try to explain."

"You done?"

"No, I'm not done."

"Well, true, she's not you friend Priscilla. She doesn't talk to me endlessly about the hotels she stays in when she travels on important corporate business, and the number of zeros in the debenture deals she's structured. She isn't afflicted with biological clock desperation. I know she's too young. What do you want me to do? Make her older? I can't."

"I want you to promise that you won't sleep with her until you know her. If you wouldn't get so intimate with women you can't possibly know yet, I wouldn't have to hear you neurotting around, moaning and groaning for endless months."

Nicky pouts, drinks from his beer.

"Neurotting around," Carla repeats.

Elsa is winding the song down. Turns out it is her handy man.

"What's juvenile diabetes?" Nicky asks abruptly.

"Why?"

"Nothing, it came up the other day, that's all."

"It's the worst. Over time more and more complications."

"But doesn't Mary Tyler Moore have it?" Nicky challenges her.

"Yeah, I think she does, actually. I think you're right."

It is crazy June weather outside; sweltering summer before its time.

The essence of Ecaterina, Nicky thinks — were he a painter, were he to try to capture her, he thinks — is a frowning face and gliding grace: so quietly poised, so self-contained, so closed behind searching India ink eyes. He wants to pierce through what contains her, and know everything.

She glides into his apartment wearing a wide-brimmed summer hat, a black sleeveless blouse, white skirt, and white tights. Her forehead beaded with perspiration, she drops her pack, smiles at the air-conditioned cool, and settles on the sofa.

"I need a cool drink," she says. He brings her a can — he has bought sugar-free soda, thinking of her — and she sips it, shaking her head. "I'm so beat," she says. "I've been running all day. We're organizing this demonstration on Eastern Europe, and it has been like crazy. Could I just rest for a while? I know we said we were going to a movie." She looks at him, waiting to know if it is OK. He says it is, and she sags face down onto the couch. "Oh man, that cool air is nice."

Nicky removes her sandals and massages her feet. A pleased look spreads across her face. Organizing demonstrations, he thinks. Half the world has been organized since he stopped paying attention, from South Africa to Nicaragua; it must be Europe's turn.

"Ummm," she says, "that feels good. I got really ripped last night." He watches her drift off to sleep. Her words bother him. Who was she with? What was she doing? He knows so little about what she does, who she is. He doesn't want to imagine her with someone else. And then he thinks it can't be good for her, doing drugs, drinking, whatever she was doing. He pushes the thought away, watching her peaceful face turned to the side on the pillow as she dozes — her half-open mouth, the tiny pool of saliva where her lips flatten against the cushion. He is pleased that she feels so comfortable with him. It seems wondrous to him that she did not exist during all the years that he was living what are now his most vivid memories — memories that scarcely seem to him to be from so long ago. And here she lies, in his life. He resolves to let this second date go without even a kiss.

She wakes, wiping her mouth. She covers her face with her hands, chuckling. "Oooh, you were watching me sleep."

Nicky bends to stroke her forehead and she reaches up to pull him to her. Caught by surprise, Nicky jerks backward.

"What's wrong?" she whispers; frowning as her fragile confidence starts to crack.

"Nothing," he says. "Absolutely nothing."

Her hesitant look is asking him, "Don't you want me?" but her little, warm hands on the back of his head keep pressing him toward her.

So much for good intentions. She is naked to the waist now. In the semi-darkness, he removes her tights. He runs his hand over her thin, firm legs.

When he is leading her into the bedroom, she asks, "Should I protect myself?"

Nicky squints down at her. It disturbs him that she puts it as a question. "Let me protect myself first," she should have said.

He stops himself from expressing the feeling. She is waiting, poised against him. "Not yet," he says. She nods, too knowingly, he thinks, and they continue walking to the bedroom, pressed tight together.

Their bodies merge together so naturally, without even a hint of first-time awkwardness. After they have made love, she lies apart from him, with her legs crossed in the air. She doesn't look at him, though he is gazing at her. She is wiggling the toes of her raised foot to the beat of a song playing on the radio.

"What?" he says.

She shakes her head a quick twitch "no."

"What?" he insists.

She squints at him now, a long moment. Then she shrugs. "I'm just trying to figure out how old you are."

She turns over, props herself up on one arm and studies him. "You have to be pretty old. I know we've both been avoiding mentioning it."

Nicky grins, relieved at first to have it out, and then not so relieved. "Would it bother you?"

"No," she hurries to say. "I like guys who are older."

"You don't want to know."

"You're not going to tell me?"

"You can figure it out from things I've told you."

"I don't care. It doesn't matter. Age doesn't mean anything."

"I agree," Nicky says, turning her over, rolling onto her, his mouth moving down from her breasts across her belly.

She places her hands between her legs, holding his mouth away. "Tell me."

His chin rests on her tightly-linked fingers; he looks up at her with his eyebrows raised. She nods and whispers, "First tell me."

Nicky sighs. "How old is daddy?"

"I told you, about forty. In September. Why?" she asks.

Nicky shrugs, smirking.

She pushes away from him and sits up rigid against the back of the bed with her knees pulled to her chest. "You can't be."

She looks precious to Nicky — all kneecaps and small, round breasts. Hard, pointy nipples spy out at him, and above, that face is all a frown, with black eyes cutting through him, and haywire hair outraged.

"Close, a few years less," he says.

She shakes her head back and forth, still with a look of shock on her face.

"I told you that you didn't want to know." He reaches up and tousles her wayward hair.

She shakes him off; ponders him. He feels scrutinized. He realizes he is very nervous that she will bolt; that this will be it.

"I knew it must be a lot," she says, musing. "I can't believe it. You sure don't look it." She giggles, her eyes moving to his erect penis. "You don't act it." She lights a cigarette and takes a long slow drag, holding the smoke in before she blows it out, shaking her head. "I can't believe you didn't tell me *first*."

"It's not a sexual disease."

A smile begins to cross her face, creasing her chin. "It's sort of neat." She sets down the cigarette and snuggles up to him. She runs her hands through his hair and buries her face between his and the pillow, flattening her cool nose against him.

Nicky dozes and wakes to find her sitting on him, with the covers over them like a tent. She is caressing his chest, singing softly to herself, "As Time Goes By." She smiles at him. "Why did Rick go to Casablanca?" she asks. She stares at him, intent on his answer.

"Why did Rick go to Casablanca?" Nicky repeats. He was probably her age when the command to play Le Marseillaise first sent goose bumps down his arms, as it still does all these years later. He stretches, groans, jiggles her body. Her little breasts swivel. "For the waters."

"But Morocco is a desert," she responds with indignation.

Nicky shrugs. "He must have been misinformed."

Ecaterina smiles, lying down on him.

When she has almost fallen asleep, he whispers in her ear, "He was looking for a job when she was only having her teeth straightened, you'll recall."

Ecaterina chuckles, and drifts off to sleep.

Nicky, having been up late with Ecaterina for too many blissful, sleepless nights in too few days is home from work, sick. "I'm old," he tells her. "The changeable weather," she tells him, mothering him through chills and fever and fever and chills; doing some grocery shopping, watching some music videos; dancing some ballet routines for him; lecturing him with vehemence on whatever atrocities are being committed in whatever Balkan country she is incensed about this week. "I burned out over Vietnam," he says. "Now I make money. Don't look so horrified. I'm old."

"You don't really mean that," she says. "This isn't Scarsdale. I don't see any wife and kids. You have not chosen the suburban life."

"No it is not Westchester, and it's not Casablanca either."

"Humph," she grunts.

She reads stories to him; cooks meals for him; sleeps with him; makes him kiss her, germs or no; drifts easily, effortlessly into domesticity.

Tonight she is in bed beside him, softly singing along with the song on the radio, lying on her stomach, her face lost in his pillow, her hand absently squeezing his thigh. Nicky finds that he doesn't buy ice cream now. He feels guilty eating it when she is with him. He mentions this to her with a laugh and she tells him seriously that he shouldn't do that. She doesn't expect it.

"Do you have to take insulin?" he asks her. He's never seen her do anything. He has been reluctant to ask questions, to pry.

"Yah," comes her soft voice from the pillow, from under her wayward tufts of hair. "Twice a day."

Nicky is crestfallen. This makes her illness so much more real. He waits, but she offers no more. She turns on her back, and with her hands under her head, she gazes at him. Her lips press tight together and relax. Those dark eyes peer into his without expression. She shrugs a shoulder, then turns on her side, away from him. Nicky begins to massage her back slowly, pressing hard, feeling her muscles, her bones, her heart beating.

"Pills?" he asks, after a long pause.

She gives her head a quick jerk no. They are silent. Then she says, "There's no such thing."

He runs his fingers slowly through her hair. He traces her delicate features, her cheeks, her little curve of a nose, its flat bridge, her protruding upper lip. He runs his hand along her arm.

"How long?" he asks. "When did you   "

"When I was fourteen."

He tries to think of her as a little girl learning to use a needle. He knows he wants to be there for her if her life gets difficult.

"It's OK," she says. "It's not so bad day-to-day. Really."

"What do you mean day-to-day?"

She shrugs, turning back over. "I don't know," she says. "Do we really have to talk about this."

"I want to know about you."

"It's just, I've had a few bad episodes. And I know things are going to start going wrong. Why are you looking like that? It doesn't matter to us, to now."

"Is that what I am? *Now*."

"You aren't suddenly going to become the suburban family type, are you?"

"Are you?"

"Not now. Not at nineteen. Could we not have this conversation?"

⚬

Ecaterina opens Nicky's apartment door with his spare key and walks in, emptying her shopping bag on the couch. He says an unintelligible hello. Nicky's voice has become a hoarse croak over the last several days. He picks up the new CD she has bought herself. He doesn't even know any of the groups she listens to.

Nicky is listening to the phone ringing at Carla's apartment. She has hung up on his obscene croak three times. She picks up and his voice comes out like a burping steer. She slams down the receiver again, while Ecaterina's body bends over in convulsions of laughter. "Would you call her for me?" he whispers. She shakes her head. "Come on, please. You don't know how frustrating this is."

"No. Try her again." When she has laughed herself out, she comes and sits on his lap, finger-combing his mussed hair.

"What do you talk about with her?" she asks curiously.

"I don't know," Nicky says. "Things. What do we talk about?"

"We don't have time to talk yet," Ecaterina says. "We're still at the just screwing stage."

"We don't just screw."

"That's true, we eat each other an awful lot."

Nicky tumbles her off his lap and wraps himself around her.

"Why do you like me?" she asks. "Really, I'm serious. I can't exactly figure it out."

"Don't try," Nicky says. You're the one, he thinks; but does not say.

Carla finally calls Nicky the next day and tells him about the pervert who harassed her the day before. Nicky, his laryngitis better, commiserates with her. "Maybe you should change your number," he offers. Ecaterina buries her head in a pillow to stifle her amusement. Nicky tells Carla he has been really sick.

She mocks, "So where is your little blonde thing? Why isn't she there?"

"She is here," Nicky protests. He is pleased to hear Carla stammer.

"So is she taking care of you?"

Nicky looks down at Ecaterina, sitting on the floor in front of him now with her hand inside his shorts. "After a fashion," he says. Ecaterina explodes.

"Is that her giggling? I'm going to throw up," Carla says.

"Ask her about Rick," Ecaterina whispers.

"What's the domestic one saying?" Carla asks.

"Nothing. She wants to know why did Rick go to Casablanca?"

"Oh, how cute. We're having such a clichéd adolescent little time together."

"You don't know."

"He was escaping from the Germans in Paris or something."

When Nicky reports her answer to Ecaterina after Carla has hung up, she has a satisfied look on her face.

"It's true," he tells her. "That was why."

She smiles with contented condescension and kisses him lightly on the cheek. "The waters," she says, and saunters off.

"I can't believe you're competing with Carla, jealous of her," Nicky says. "You're such an adorable, cute little thing." He reaches after her, but she breaks away.

"I don't want to be someone's cute little girl," she says.

Nicky stands still, taken by surprise. "But you are little," he says, "you're barely five feet." He holds his hands apart in the air to show little, and makes an apologetic, pouting face.

"I want to be equal, like you and Carla are when you talk." She stands in the middle of the room, shoulders limp, mouth open, India ink eyes riveting him; her whole being frowning at him. "Life is all new to me. I want someone to share that with."

"Cat – don't. *You* are new to me." He again holds his hands up, about a foot apart from each other. "Little," he mouths.

She smiles at him finally. Giggles. Her little, perfect, braces-straightened teeth he so rarely sees. He runs his hand through her fly-away hair.

"I love you," he tells her. "I just love you." She purses her lips shyly and turns her eyes downward. "And *that* is new," he says.

⊶◉⊷

After the conversation with Carla, Nicky has not seen Ecaterina in half a week, the longest separation since the first day he laid eyes on her. She went home to her parents for several days and made plans with her school friends for most of the past weekend. She told him she needed to come up for air, and he knew he should not press her. He also needs to make up for lost time at work. He doesn't known when he will see her. He left that up to her, and feels bereft each day.

She appears at his door without calling. Surprise turns instantly to soaring joy. Before her bag hits the floor, they are embracing. Before either of them speaks a word they are on the living room rug, naked, straining at bodily barriers that keep them from being one. Writhing in frustration with their inability to get further in at any opening, they moan together as Nicky explodes inside her body.

Ecaterina lies on the floor, stroking his head, all the while scowling. "I didn't want to do that. I told myself we would just talk tonight. We don't ever talk."

"We're still at the fucking stage."

"But why don't we get to the next stage?"

"Do you know how many married people would give everything for the kind of intensity we feel, and all you want to do is douse it."

"Well, could we go out? I'm just going to hate myself if we screw all night."

He ponders her. "I'll take you to hear Elsa."

The decorations from July 4th and Thanksgiving and Christmas and New Year's somehow never got taken down. Elsa is pounding on the keys in the smoky darkness.

"Maybe she'll do some of the hot Bessie Smith songs," Nicky says to Ecaterina, as they sit on stools beside the piano.

"Who?"

"Bessie Smith."

"I'm not as old as you."

Nicky looks over at her and groans. She meets his gaze resolutely. He says, "I'm not *that* old, for Christ sake. Bessie Smith was in the Thirties, or maybe it was the Twenties!"

Nicky turns to Elsa. "Play 'Kitchen Man,' Elsa."

Old Elsa, frumpy in her lavender blouse and black skirt, shudders as her fingers continue to work the keys. Her chocolate brown face creases into a lumpy frown. "Honey, you know I can't do that at this hour of the night. What would this nice lady here say. Got to ease into those songs." Elsa chuckles. "Ah the music lovers around here."

She slides into "Ain't Misbehaving."

The crowd ebbs and flows, becomes older and younger, preppier and hipper. The beer bottles clink. The smoke clings. The hours pass. Ten becomes twelve becomes one. Nicky senses that Ecaterina is uneasy. All at once she is squeezing his wrist. He turns to her.

"I really love you so much," she whispers abruptly.

Nicky opens his mouth, about to reply.

"It just seems," she continues, "so inappropriate."

Nicky takes a swig from his beer bottle, holding it to his lips for a long moment. He sets the bottle down softly then. "Inappropriate. Cat! Like wearing a wrong tie, like out-of-style pants, like setting a fork on the wrong side, like belching in public."

Elsa is singing "As Time Goes By."

Ecaterina has her hand on Nicky's neck. "I really want you. I do." He sighs, lets her hand pull his face to hers. She kisses him as Elsa sings.

He feels that his cheek is becoming wet. Her hands hold him, keep him kissing her as she trembles. And then she lets him go. Wiping her face dry, she squints at Nicky, her eyes swollen, her lips pressed tightly together. When at last she speaks, she says, "I'm sorry. I just felt so sad. I always had this romantic dream of sitting in a place like this kissing to 'As Time Goes By.'"

"So why are you crying?"

Her eyes well up again. "The timing," she mouths. She peers up at him, not letting him look away, scrutinizing his eyes, hers asking him if he understands what she is saying.

Elsa's voice is soothing. Nicky thinks that she is the one eternal in his universe. In the smoky darkness, in the timeless, ageless saloon with Elsa, he can sit, and marinate his ache.

Was it all a flight of fancy, a mirage of sweltering heat, a chimera of chills and fever. Her rational analysis of the situation, delivered in the Sheridan Square station as train after train rattled past, was unfailingly accurate.

"Why can't you see it! We are at different stages. You want a wife, no you don't even. You want to be married without being married. I'm not ready for you yet. It's not time for me to settle down. I'm only nineteen years old; don't you understand? You are my father's age. My father's age. I do love you, I do. These days have been, like wonderful, like incredible. But it isn't real. It isn't that wonderful in real life! It isn't."

"But this is real life. What are you talking about?"

"It isn't."

"We fill each other up. There is no you, no me. We engulf each other."

"I know we do. Don't you see? That's just it. I have to protect myself."

"From what?" Nicky screamed in frustration, the sound drowned in the roar of the oncoming Number One train.

She pressed her head into his chest, rubbing her nose against him, wrapping her arms around him one last, one final — he knew it, he knows it, and his eyes are wet with grief and his fists are clenched with frustration — time.

Nicky tries to tell himself there will be others; there are always others. When he finishes mourning, they will come, from some unexpected place, but they will come. He'll go out with a woman with whom he can share a pint of ice cream, sitting on the couch on a rainy Sunday, he and she with the frosty pint on one of their laps, and each dipping a spoon into the sweetness.

He becomes aware of the merry, boisterous crowd around him calling out. He looks up at the faces glowing with fun, as Elsa bangs out a familiar melody. Another of her favorite hot ones called "Stick It Where You Stuck It Last Night." She likes to sing the song for newlyweds. Elsa's own special kind of blessing. Nicky looks around and spies out the young couple, holding hands and looking embarrassed. They aren't regulars.

He finds himself tapping his fingers on the counter, forgetting for a moment his gloom, as Elsa pulls the microphone close, and teases out the final verse.

And all of the music lovers, all the sodden, late-night regulars who've heard her do this a hundred times in the early morning of a hundred lonely nights, roar.

Nicky thinks about Ecaterina. She will be going to sleep now. In her room in her parents' home, or at a friend's dorm room, or in the arms of some boy she doesn't know very well. And wherever she is, she will be in a bathroom with her needle and her little bottle, making it possible for her to reach the next morning. He drinks from his bottle of beer. The frost has loosened the label and it is sliding off under his fingers. He will miss her and he will stop missing her — at least, he tells himself he will — but she will be out there, going on. He feels a sorrow, a kind of helpless sadness he has not known before.

Carla's hand is on his neck. "Hi, sorry I'm late. Elsa's back to her old favorite again, huh? Where's the happy couple?"

Nicky points at the smiling man and woman, the newlyweds. "Ah."

She sits down heavily beside him and frowns into his eyes. "How are you doing?" she asks. "Are you OK?"

Wanda

I F LAW SCHOOLS DIDN'T do everything alphabetically, I would never have known Wanda. Women might concede that Wanda was plain, but few men would be that charitable, especially with the limp that sent her right hip thrusting out drunkenly with every step she took. As I say, if it hadn't been for the first letter of her last name, I would never have even met her.

I know that this admission forever marks me as the insensitive, superficial male incarnate for some women. I can even hear my gentle old grandmother drawing her moral, "And how much less rich your life would have been if you had not met her." As it happens, though, law schools seat first-year students alphabetically and she was next to me on the left. We soon became close; friends in the affliction of the law, haunting the coffee shops around the university, talking torts and interpleaders and the dissent in *Palsgraf.*

After law school, we moved to Park Avenue law firms, effortlessly, as a matter of course. All of New York was on the fast track in those days, and the money the firms were paying us made us think we were something special.

We met often for lunch, and when we happened to be working late — which was almost always — and the client was therefore paying, we met for those dinners that made us feel so much a part of the New York scene. It was only with Wanda of all my friends and co-workers that there was even a hint of a dark lining to our silver cloud.

On a brisk late fall evening, we planned to meet for dinner at nine. But I had a last minute crisis on a deal, and phoned Wanda to cancel. She said she would finish up her backlog of time sheets and wait for me. I called the steak place to ask how late we could get there, and they said eleven-fifteen. By the time I got to Wanda's office, it was close, so we had to really move. She hopped along beside me out to the street and we took a cab the few short blocks. When we arrived, adrenaline flowing, at eleven-thirteen, the maître d' first shook his head, then shrugged and seated us.

After ordering, we sat back and both sighed at the same time. We laughed; then we began to decompress, letting the incessant poundings of the day float away. Wanda ordered us wine. Wanda was heavily into oenophilia, her word. She chose us a Chardonnay. When the waiter just naturally offered me the approval, I pointed to her. She did the whole number, swirling it, sniffing it, tasting it, and nodding almost imperceptibly. She looked at me and pointed to the label."Great year for the Napa Chardonnays," she said as we clinked glasses.

I noticed Wanda's bushy eyebrows drawn tight. I asked what was up. "I'm in the dog house," she murmured, and scratched her head in silence. Her hair had been long and curly when we were in law school — a red cyclone. One day, after we had been working for half a year or so she had it cut short and swept back — very clean and conservative. I thought it was awful. Whatever earthy sex there had been in her was coiffed out. Maybe I shouldn't have said anything, but I really thought she ought to have a man's opinion. She retorted that I was a sexist; that I just liked little girls with long hair; if I grew up I'd see what women were all about. She was, of course, describing the woman who had sat alphabetically to the right of me in law school, the woman I was seeing, and, by the way, her good friend. I let it pass. It was not a serious rebuke. It was more a rote political statement, some version of which I heard regularly from her, whether directed at me or another offending male. If directed at another, I agreed heartily, "What an asshole." Routine chatter.

Wanda drank more wine before she explained why she was in the doghouse. "We had reviews today." Her freckled face was losing the initial flush the wine had given it. She took a gulp, but the freckles stood out still more blotchy on her pasty white skin. "Roger wrote me a really bad review."

"You're kidding."

"No. That's just it. It was out of the blue. I don't think he realized how bad it sounded."

"What did he say?"

"Oh, he doesn't think I'm serious-minded enough. You know, nothing stuff."

"But that's crazy. You must bill more hours than anyone, the way you're always working late."

She took another sip of wine and cocked her head. "A little bitter; strong aftertaste. Not bad though."

I felt as if we both knew they were beginning to pave the way for the inevitable. Obviously, they wouldn't say to her, "Sorry but clients don't feel quite secure with an attorney who can't walk straight; of course, if you were a more attractive gal they might feel protective and drawn to your disability, but what can we do? The people we make partners have to be appealing to clients. Clients are our money. But we're happy to bury you in a back room and let you churn out brilliant research for a few more years."

"He walks in and sees me on the phone or people in my office. He doesn't see me still there at midnight working, because he's gone home. I mean I'm very social; I am. But I stay late to get the work done."

I nodded.

"When I went to him, he downplayed the review, but – "

"Well, so don't worry."

"He likes my work; he said that."

"So maybe you just ought to be more careful about appearances — look like you're working hard."

She gave reassured nods and I smiled comfortingly. Into the terrible stillness that hung over our table, she snorted, and then boomed out, "Guess who wriggled his way over last night." Her coal-lump eyes were suddenly aglow.

"Wendell the Weasel." I stated the obvious.

"You — guessed it," she said with a peculiar mid-sentence pause that provided her speech its own unique rhythmic gusto.

She loved to tell me, with equal parts of scorn, bravado and amusement, about her midweek, late-night adventures with this mysterious Lord Byron, who was surely unaware of the feral name Wanda had given him. I cannot decide whether or not he existed.

Wendell, she had explained, was the boyfriend of a rather voluptuous friend of her sister's. Wendell was a week-night phenomenon who seemed to appear every two or three weeks when he approached the end of a work day and realized he had reached the limits of monogamy. Wanda enjoyed telling me lustily of these illicit and entirely mechanical encounters. She expressed utter contempt for him — "typical male cheat" — and savored every minute of her victory over her sister's friend.

"Was it wonderfully orgasmic?" I asked.

"Not — at — all," Wanda said, ecstatically hoisting her wine glass. "Umm." Her eyes flashed anew and she continued. "I told him — not tonight. I sent him — wriggling on his way. Whew!"

"I don't believe it."

"I couldn't — be bothered," she chuckled with satisfaction. "I was reading — *The Iliad*. My new cultural project."

"I love it."

"He needs to be put in his place. After all — a classic. I mean really. No time for Weasels."

As it happened, Wanda had a further agenda item for our dinner meeting. His name was David something, and he was no Weasel. He was Beer Commercial. And Wanda made no pretense of her bafflement. Though he worked on her floor, she had never before spoken to him more than formally and politely, and all of a sudden one day he stopped her to chat, and then called her and asked her to a movie. What did it mean, she wanted to know. They had gone to the movie. "And that's all," she said, her palms out, her mouth open, her neck thrust forward in a silent expression of amazement. "Explain," her frown commanded me.

"Well," I said, "Did he kiss you good night?"

"He shook my hand!" She laughed her big chesty guffaw that sent her neck thrusting forward even further. "I mean really!"

I asked whether he paid for her at the theater. "Are you kidding? I wouldn't permit that."

"Well, did he offer?"

"I whipped out my bills before we were up to the box office."

"You make this very difficult."

The restaurant had mostly emptied out. Two men in three-piece suits were leaning toward each other speaking in low tones. The listener was taking short, sucking puffs of his cigarette and blowing the smoke out hard. I was somehow annoyed when words like "prospectus" and "S-16" and "the '33 Act" floated our way. Impossible to get away from this stuff.

It was well after midnight when we left, tired, talked out. We walked west and north through the now quiet canyons. A bum was peeing against the Citicorp Building. I was thinking how devastated Wanda must be by her review. She was a creature of her law firm, finding, I thought, her whole stability in its people and its mythology. Her very being was about becoming a partner. It seemed so unfair. She was a brilliant anti-trust lawyer. After walking off the dinner, we hailed a cab uptown. "Don't go through the park," Wanda told the driver. Which route was shorter was a debate we rehashed by rote on a regular basis. This night, I said nothing.

⸻◆⸻

Winter was in the air now. I could see my breath, and I was wearing gloves most of the time. Walking briskly by a florist in the rush hour throng, I thought about getting Maggie something. Maggie was that little girl with long hair who had sat to the right of me in law school. A block later, I decided to go back. I picked up a bunch of freesia for her. We both loved their light, room-filling perfume.

When I got home, Maggie was running the bath water. She smiled at the freesia, which I put in a vase, as I heard her splash into the tub full of bubbles. She sat soaking, reading over a brief she had to finish. I cleaned the mess from the last night's take-out Chinese dinner. We went through crazy periods when we were both working late. If we saw the apartment for half an hour at night it was a lot.

"Alan," she called to me.

I wandered in, stuck my foot in the suds and ran it along her leg, then sat down on the edge of the tub and told her the latest Weasel news, and about Wanda's review.

"Do you think the Weasel exists?" she asked.

"Sure. Don't you?"

"I don't know. I guess so."

"Well?"

She just looked at me.

"Maybe he likes her soul," I offered. "Aren't you always telling me that's what is important?"

She answered with a snort.

"What are you thinking?"

"You wouldn't like me if I limped."

"I'm actually very kinky."

She threw suds at me.

Then her mood seemed to change. She threw her brush into the water angrily.

"What?"

"It pisses me off. If it were a man who limped, it wouldn't stand in the way of his making partner. They would favor him. The clients would look up to him, thinking it was a war injury."

Not many weeks later, it was smoky and steamy in the restaurant, and the chill of winter evening did not quite leave me because we were in a draft at the window. Wanda was complimenting herself on the choice of the brie. I told her I liked the wine and she said, "Yeah, they make a great Zin."

Wanda was worrying about her leg. We hadn't talked about it much since law school. What was there to say? She knew she limped. I knew she limped. When we were ambling along Columbus Avenue on our many exploratory ventures into the new restaurants that sprang up weekly, I invariably found myself on the wrong side of her — the side she listed toward — and spent half a block finding a subterfuge to switch sides without embarrassing her.

The candle on our table flickered when the draft hit it, causing a thin stream of dark smoke to shoot upward. A patch of ice stretched across the sidewalk just outside. I found myself more and more attentive to the approach of pedestrians, anticipating the bizarre bodily contortions that resulted when feet hit the slick spot. Women giggled as they righted themselves. Men glanced furtively into the window to see if they had been caught out, and hurried on without expression. Wanda said I was guilty of sexist stereotyping. I denied it, so we watched for a while. Being lawyers, we disputed niceties, but in the end she conceded. About then a hand-holding couple hit the spot and their joined hands shot above their heads as if they were victors accepting plaudits. She took a furtive peek in the window. He giggled. I shrugged.

Wanda was saying, "Orthopedists only want to cut. You walk in the door and they say, 'Scalpel.' I went a couple of years ago to have my leg looked at. He was ready to put me right in the hospital and start slicing. I asked him what the chances of success were; he said good. I asked if that meant I would be able to walk correctly and he said probably not." She laughed her deep, chesty, incredulous laugh — mouth open, eyes big, neck forward. "I mean really!"

She sipped her wine. "Just another lame lawyer," she said. We were both silent for a time. She looked down at the table, now bashful with the intimacy. I felt uncomfortable. I listened to snatches from the next table. Two young women were leaning forward in intense conversation, each with one elbow propped on the table, cigarette hand poised above. I could hear only a few stray words. Orgasm. Oral. Clitoral. It seemed as if the particular mix of steamy heat and cold air currents transmitted the o-r sound most effectively.

I didn't speak to Wanda for over a week after that. I had been drafted into working on an unfriendly tender offer, so I was eating lunch in and ordering dinner from the deli. I'd had about three hours of sleep a night.

Wanda called me at the office one morning and said it was important — hot news — so I said I'd try to get away for lunch.

She was waiting in line when I arrived. I ordered a hamburger with Jarlsberg cheese. She ordered a spinach quiche and salad with vinaigrette, but she didn't come out with her news.

For dessert, I seduced Wanda into having the chocolate fondue, and we were sitting there moaning in ecstasy as we dipped pineapple and banana and pound cake slices into deep rich steaming chocolate.

"So what is your news?" I asked finally. Her grin told me she had been enjoying keeping me waiting.

"Oh ho," she said. "The big — score."

"David? The bankruptcy guy? You're kidding." I could see the satisfaction my surprise gave her.

"No — for real. Can you believe it?" And then she let loose with the story. "He called me up yesterday and said there was a really fantastic jazz group playing last night — did I want to go? I was thinking, hell no, it won't start till eleven o'clock and by the time it's over he'll — shake my hand again and that'll be it. I mean really!

"I said I had to get to work the next morning for an eight o'clock departmental breakfast. That was actually true. With Roger, breakfast means a powdered doughnut and coffee from the canteen. So I told him I couldn't really do it. And he said he wanted to see me, so why didn't we just go out to dinner instead." She paused and raised her eyebrows. "We were both working late enough to charge it, so we went to this French place. Oohhh the mousse was — almost more orgasmic than what happened later. Anyhow, afterwards, he takes me home in a taxi, and of course I invited him up. We talked a while and he kept starting to leave and I couldn't believe he took a taxi up just to take a taxi back down — I mean when did you last escort someone home in New York? And then he shook my hand goodbye and I wasn't going to have that again so I kissed him — and after that he seemed to remember what to do." She let out a guffaw then. "You can bet I didn't hear a word Roger said this morning. Exhaustion. I mean I am — sore. I didn't know I had so many muscles.

"Afterwards, he broke into confessional, telling me about his girlfriend (my heart sinking) and how they are having trouble and they talked it over and decided they ought to see other people and he asked me out that first time, but then when the big moment of truth came he got — cold feet. And he would have gotten cold feet this time again, but I pushed him — over the edge." She stopped, tipped her head back, and drained her glass of wine. And then she asked me point blank, "So what do you think? Will I see him again?" She smirked, twisting her hands around the empty glass of wine.

I sat back in my counseling-clients manner and surveyed the situation. "I'm sure you will," I said.

And then she abruptly changed the topic. "Do you think my review is the kiss of death? Tell me the truth." She looked down at the table, played her finger in a wet spot. "I'm good enough to make partner." She looked up at me hard. She ran a finger along the edge of the chocolate pot and licked it.

I nodded. That was certainly true, But I did not think it was the kind of truth that mattered.

As if reading my mind, she said, with bitterness in her voice, "What if I didn't limp?"

I thought for a moment about what to answer, but she was already moving on. Maggie's brother was getting married, and that led to a bunch of wedding-preparation questions, dresses and flowers and so forth, that did not interest me at all. Then we somehow got talking about a friend of hers at work named Charley who had the bad luck to get himself assigned to a real bitch named Abigail. Wanda was smiling, telling me how Charley had thrown up his hands, made as if he were strangling himself, and sank into his chair; only it rolled back and he fell onto the floor. She laughed heartily. After that we were silent, working on the last of the banana slices.

Then she said practically in a whisper, "I'm going into the hospital next week."

"Hospital," I said. "Why?"

After a few more banana slices dripping with chocolate, she explained. "I decided to have the operation. The big-time one. It might really work. Really."

I had just failed to express my true thoughts to my friend twice in barely five minutes. I could not quite manage it a third time. "Have you thought about getting a second opinion?" I asked. "Is it too late to do that?" I tried to put urgency in my voice. A hedge, at least, but a weak response that did not make me feel a lot better.

Gridlock

I N THE SPRING THAT year, the subways and the buses all stopped running. The whole city became a bit tipsy, and none of us felt as pressed as we usually did by the partners' unreasonable deadlines. Well, none of us except Charley anyhow. We were quite taken with the new word that entered the vocabulary of the city that April amid dire warnings and tv interviews with traffic flow experts. And of course Mayor Koch had plenty to say. The new word was *Gridlock*. We were sort of rooting for the phenomenon itself. River to river, Ninety-Sixth Street to Fourteenth Street. Absolute and complete immobility. Nothing budging. Charley maintained it simply was not possible. Wanda was more intrigued with how they would undo it if it did really happen. Everyone expected a long strike, so all bets were off.

We were in Wanda's office, arguing about when you could say a true rather than an apparent gridlock had been reached. We had descended already to nice distinctions, lawyerly distinctions. Wanda had a view down Park Avenue toward the Pan Am building, and traffic sure was jammed up. But every couple of minutes the cars did inch forward half a length. Ah hah, not true gridlock.

When the new guy, Darryl, stuck his head in the door, wanting to know how to go about getting pencils sharpened — "Just put them in your outbox," Charlie rushed to be the font of knowledge — Wanda quickly invited him to join us. He was a lateral transfer from another firm, a few years ahead of us.

"I did that," he said with a wry smile on his face. "But they never came back sharpened."

We laughed and told him how that worked, as Wanda made introductions.

"Darryl Hilton," It was not lost on me that she had made sure to meet him already. "Charley Daich and Nicky Smith. Or did you run across them already? They're in Corporate, like you. I'm in the Antitrust Department, I think I mentioned."

"Yes, I remember," he said.

He had a sleepy smile, but a solid handshake. And sapphire cuff links on an obviously expensive shirt. I'm no expert, but his gray suit looked custom-made to me. More than his clothing and his sudden arrival in the firm struck me as odd. In any case, Wanda could not take her eyes off him.

We all watched out the window for a while, not saying much, gazing off at the stagnant stream of yellow taxi roofs below. In our thermo-sealed world, no horns blared. The moment was conducive to daydreams, and I, of course, dreamed of my restaurant. Today it was Nicky's Country Inn I conjured. I was obsessing on it. Anything to blot out the memory, the pain, Ecaterina's face in my head. Wanda dreamed, well, she was pretty open that she was not planning to wait for her biological clock to wind down. She was forever honey-hunting, as she put it. She was certainly focused and persistent. So far, no sticky honey had clung, but here was quite a potful, God protect him. As for Charley — Charley I couldn't imagine thinking about anything else but becoming a partner at this prestigious law firm five years from now. Maybe he would. Maybe his dream was more real than ours were. As for mine, I didn't think I would ever truly have the guts to break out and do it.

The spell was broken, really more like smashed than broken, when a head poked in the door. Mid-back-length auburn hair flowed forward as shoulders leaned in. Hand with long, glossy red fingernails clawed the jamb. Something between a scowl and a frown creased the face. "Charley, I need to see you now." She waited a beat. "If you can spare the time."

Charley jumped up. "Of course," he said, hurrying out, tucking in his shirt, feeling to see if his tie was straight, pulling his jacket down where it had bunched up.

Darryl looked at me with an amused, questioning cock of his head.

"That," I said, "was her ladyship Abigail Swarthmore. No time for chitchat. Or even a hello to us mortals."

"She's quite attractive," Darryl noted, more of an aesthetic aside than an expression of desire.

Wanda was quick to add, "She's a total bitch. Like ice. She is about at your level, and Charley has to work for her sometimes. He is popping Tums the whole time."

I chuckled at the thought. "And by the way, if you plan to stay here till your partnership year, you better hope there are at least two openings. Abby's a given, a shoe-in: incredibly smart, politically savvy, dare I add ruthless."

Wanda made sure to interject, "She has a boyfriend." And then commented, "Amazingly enough."

"Oh, that's a story there," I said. "You tell it."

Wanda lowered her voice. "It is kind of unbelievable. She never talks to anyone about her personal life, but one day Mitchell's old secretary — he had taken her to lunch at a fancy French place — spotted Abigail at a shall I say secluded table, all cozy and kissy with a guy. Not at all like the Abigail we know. I mean, really, it was like they were about to do it at the table, the way Jennifer told it."

I cut in, "And what is more crazy, this guy was so un-Abby-like, I don't know how to describe it..."

"Scruffy." Wanda said firmly. "Like long hair, jeans, a work shirt. Not even nice jeans; old and rumpled. Like he was still in the Sixties. I'm surprised they let him in a place like that."

"Abby's a regular there; brings clients all the time; the staff fawn all over her, seeing dollar signs; she could bring a bag lady and they would smile and nod."

"He was certainly not corporate. By the way." Wanda turned to Darryl. "Don't ever call her Abby to her face. She will freak. She will rip out your balls," Wanda said in her enthusiasm, then looked embarrassed. She shook her head, thinking about the scene at the restaurant. "Everyone was whispering about it, but we never found out any more."

"No more sightings?" Darryl asked.

"Not a one. Zero."

When I got back to the office I shared with Charley, I saw that my secretary, who lived in Brooklyn, had finally swung in. I looked at my watch. Eleven o'clock. She glared at me with an intensity that said if my mouth even opened, I was a dead man. The words that she actually spit out of her mouth were, "I left my house at five-thirty a.m."

I escaped into the office only to find Charley frantic. The phone slammed just as I stepped in. His pudgy face was beet red.

"What is it?" I asked.

He sneered. Shuffled through the mound of papers strewn across his desk. He always insisted he knew exactly where everything was. Dialed another number.

"What do you mean, you don't know where the messenger is?" he screamed shrilly into the phone. "Mr. Mitchell has to have it right away for a very important transaction. Now. This minute.

We told you this was a super-rush. What do you mean, don't I know what's going on? We have a closing. Vice presidents from two big banks managed to get here." He slammed the phone down and sat staring at his papers.

Through that crazy first week, each day the office cleared out at three o'clock. Secretaries, word processors, mail room staff, librarians, and even lawyers had to be ready to go when their carpools or cab pools were ready to leave for New Jersey or Long Island or Westchester or Queens or Brooklyn. Everything was organized. For once, the work waited. Of course the work was stuck in traffic too, as Charley had learned. I was in no hurry to leave the office. Living right in Manhattan, I was barely inconvenienced. I waited for the grid to unlock and took a late taxi home.

All week, Wanda was calling me regularly with Darryl updates. "Nick, Darryl had lunch with me. I can't believe the things he says he has in his house. You know that Munch litho in his office? It's real. I mean, really, do you believe?" Or again, "Nick, Darryl lives in a brownstone in Brooklyn he *bought* when he moved here. Bought, just like that. He says it's in a pretty marginal neighborhood, bur still. I tried hinting that I would love to see it. Silence. No response at all. I can't read him. He seems so happy to see me; I mean, he's really friendly. But nothing." And a few days later, "I heard Darryl talking to Sally, the receptionist on twenty-three who does tickets. He was checking prices for Haiti. Haiti of all places." She lowered her voice. "Two tickets. What the fuck."

Charley, in his way, was equally mesmerized by Darryl. Smug doesn't do justice to the way he looked one afternoon when he walked into our office, as always in suit jacket and vest, beaming at me. "I had lunch with Darryl," he announced. He had that look whenever one of the senior associates, or God help us, partners, asked him to lunch: "I went for Italian with Jack Wilson" was supposed to leave me certain Charley was on the partnership track. But Darryl was too new to count, and not even very senior. There was just something about him.

For me that week, the mornings were a special joy. The days were sunny and warm. Where I lived, on Eighty-Ninth Street off Central Park West, the faint scent of the country blew off the park. Birds twittered. I bounded out of bed before the alarm. It struck me as I did it that first time that *bounding* was what I was actually doing. I was eager for the long hike, which turned out to take an hour. It was a moving festival. Bicycles spinning along, roller skaters darting in and out. Women in skirts or dresses and sneakers, men in suits and ties and running shoes. And so many smiles.

A few days later, I heard that the police were blockading the roads at Ninety-Sixth Street. No cars with fewer than three riders were permitted downtown. A boon to the would be passenger class, of which I quickly became a member. After that, I walked up seven blocks, waited on an impromptu line, as driver-only cars rolled up looking for riders, and rode downtown as far as the congestion permitted.

Now even Marge Donnelly, old Frozen Hair, was raving about Darryl. He had broken through some negotiating impasse on her deal. I told Darryl what she said.

"Oh really?" he replied, shrugging it off with those sleepy eyes. "I did that kind of deal once in Chicago."

I was sitting in his office, with my feet up on his second chair, squinting at the Munch on his wall. It was *Evening on Karl Johan Street*. I had seen the oil version a couple of years earlier at a big Munch exhibit. It loomed up there: a ghostly throng of faceless clones hunching down the street.

"How did you get that?" I asked. Munchs are hardly ever even available."

"Oh, a friend gave it to me. It's just a print," he mumbled.

I stared into his hazel eyes. "Really? Wanda thought you told her it was an original."

He laughed.

All the typewriters had gone quiet. I looked at my watch. Two thirty. The world was unmoored. I squinted at Darryl, with his eyes now cast down on the pencil in his hand. He twisted it with his fingers.

His secretary came in to say she was leaving. He gave her the letter he had been drafting and asked her to type it before she left. She expressed her annoyance and he said evenly, "Well, you know, we still do have to work; this is a law firm." She snapped the letter from him and went, muttering that she was going to miss her ride. Not everyone, it seemed was as charmed as we were by Darryl.

Charley happened by, heard my voice, and not to be left out of anything, poked his pudgy face in the door. "Mr. Smith. Mr. Hilton. There's work to be done here. This is no place for levity, idle chatter." He came fully in and closed the door. After ten minutes of idle chatter, Charley bowed out of Darryl's office. Literally. But he often did that.

Now only the occasional ring of a phone broke the silence. I could not seem to get moving. Something about the silence made work seem far off. Darryl sighed. "This is getting to me," he said. I hadn't realized that he was coming in at six with the rest of the organized Brooklyn crowd. "I'm going to be here till midnight," he added. He smiled. "Marge Donnelly is doing another deal."

"F.H. won't let go of you once she's latched on," I told him. He frowned questioningly. "Frozen Hair," I explained. He thought about it and smiled.

For some reason, in that afternoon gone silent, I started to confide my restlessness to Darryl. I had never spoken of my desires to anyone here but Wanda. I was not wrong to trust Darryl though. He didn't laugh at the idea of giving up all the dollars to become an innkeeper. He actually encouraged me to look into it. He agreed that the dewy mornings and birds sure beat the car fumes and stress. My enthusiasm grew and I started talking a mile a minute. Then I came to finances and sort of sputtered out.

He looked at me with an incredulous grin. "Aren't you a corporate lawyer?" he asked.

I just stared at him.

"Leverage it," he said. "Leverage is like magic."

"What if it fails?" I asked.

He shrugged. "What do your clients do if a venture fails?"

"Suffer."

"Wrong answer." He shook his head. "OPM."

"Other people's money." I fell silent.

By the third week, the strike had become simply part of the routine of life. Loretta, Mitchell's new secretary, whose high squeaky voice and bouncy boobs set off by tight sweaters were an endless source of fascination to us, had returned to talking about shoes, and sweaters of course. We liked it when she contemplated a new sweater.

I was barely concentrating on work. I spent half the day with my door closed, on the phone investigating financing, and at night studying. I was getting closer and closer to the inn's becoming real. Then I had moments when I just couldn't believe it was happening; Wanda's raised eye brows and "Well, I don't know" kept bringing me down. But soon enough I would speak with Darryl and his matter-of-fact acceptance would get me going again.

Friday night we went out for a drink and dinner after work, Wanda, Charley, Darryl and I. A little Italian restaurant Wanda knew on Thompson Street. Darryl said he needed some money, so we stopped at the ChemBank machine.

Darryl inserted his card and tapped in the wrong numbers. The machine informed him that it was sorry, but he'd better try again. Squinting into the starry sky he said, "Oh yeah, it must be eight six at the end." Tapped that in. "How many shots do you get, I wonder?" Wanda said as Darryl frowned at the second rejection. He said, "Oh, I better call home. I have the number written down there. This is a new card."

Wanda and I looked at each other wide-eyed. The machine continued whirring away and Charley said, "You better hurry. I think it only gives you so may seconds before it keeps the card."

Darryl ran over to a phone booth on the corner and talked on the phone. Then he stood waiting as we gawked. Someone at home? Wanda was beside herself, and not able to say anything.

Darryl at the phone booth laughed and held his palm out in the air helplessly Then he was talking again and Charley yelled, "Hurry up, hurry up, it's starting to go."

"Can't you cancel the transaction?" Wanda asked.

Charley scanned the machine. "I can't see how. Someone graffitied it."

Darryl ran back in time to hear the machine gurgle and churn and then go silent, as the screen printed out the information that he could pick up his card between the hours of nine and five, Monday thru Friday.

"Do you think I could borrow twenty dollars?" he asked us. Charley flipped out an instant crisp twenty-dollar bill.

"Thanks," Darryl said sheepishly.

At dinner, none of us asked who he had talked to. Not sure why we felt as if it were a taboo subject. We had somehow created the taboo out of thin air. We chattered on about the law firm, about gridlock, about Abigail and her boyfriend.

Around eleven, Darryl said he ought to get going because he had to come in Saturday. F.H.'s closing was on Monday and he had reserved ten hours of word processing time for documents he had yet to prepare for the word processors. We said good night and he left.

As the waiter cleared the dessert dishes and asked if we wanted more coffee, we sat silently. But the moment he finished pouring, Wanda and Charley exploded. "Who was he calling?" "Why is there someone at home?" "Does he have a girlfriend after all?" "No wonder he never made a move." "Why didn't he ever mention her?"

"You know," I said, considering as I spoke, "if you think about it, he has never told us a thing about himself. We all talk and he listens."

"It doesn't make sense," Charley said. "If he has someone at home, why is he always so willing to spend his evenings with us. And this is Friday night after all."

"Maybe she works nights."

"She was home."

"Right. We don't even know it is a woman?" I said.

"A child?" Charley asked.

We both looked at him. Then we sat silently sipping our coffee.

"No way," Wanda blurted out.

Saturday, I went for a long walk in Central Park. Walked and walked, lost in contemplation, fear, uncertainty. I sat on the cliff next to the castle looking out over the flying kites and the bicycles and roller skates and ball games. Could I really just leave all this? Most everyone wanted to, but the money trapped us. Ulcers came, heart attacks came, but no one could imagine giving up the money.

I heard on someone's transistor radio that the city caved in and the union ordered the transit workers back. As I walked home I already saw buses everywhere. They looked so ungainly, so out of place, strange and cumbersome and foreign. I felt an inexplicable sadness. The end was too sudden. Back to business as usual. It seemed so extravagant, almost decadent, to be able to hop a bus or subway and just go — anywhere, freely.

Monday morning, I took the subway to work. I slipped the token in the slot; it felt odd to be doing it, and at the same time so normal. I got in at my usual ten. I poured a cup of coffee and stopped by Darryl's office. I wanted to run some new restaurant ideas by him, but his office was dark. The crowd on Karl Johan Street peered down at me from their gloom. I remembered Darryl had F.H.'s closing this morning, but Loretta squeaked that he hadn't been in. F. H. was frantic having to go it alone. I checked back at eleven-thirty but he was just not in. Wanda called me and opened with, "What the fuck?" She added, "He was home Saturday. Or someone was." She went on to say she had called his number Saturday morning from a phone booth just to see who answered. A male answered. "Maybe it's a visitor?" she asked hopefully.

In the afternoon there were a series of partners' meetings, The whole executive committee was in the twenty-fifth floor conference room, Loretta told me with that air of "I know more than I'm telling." Even after the meeting, Mitchell was unavailable most of the day and I needed his OK on a subordinated debenture I was drafting for him.

Tuesday morning, I was at my desk at ten o'clock, and spent two dreary, deadlocked hours on the phone with an associate at Dagner, Smithfield, quibbling over terms of the debenture indenture. "Dagner, Smithfield indentures always say it this way," he told me flatly. He managed to seem taken aback when I told him that ours didn't. We wrangled over that paragraph for ten minutes, but we both knew we were at an impasse. So eventually we moved on. And line by line, word by word in places, we worked our way to lunch time.

Charley was waiting impatiently to tell me the first shocker when I hung up. I saw the inane cherubic grin on his face, and knew he had some really juicy gossip that he would only spill when he thought I was frustrated enough.

"What?" I asked with my annoyance showing enough for him to get to the point.

"Darryl is gone."

"What?" I asked.

There was no more. I went out in the hall with Charley and we questioned Loretta, who proclaimed self-importantly that "It's personal." We finally went to Mitchell himself, who reassured us. But his job was to be reassuring. "We expect him back shortly."

Something didn't fit. I had become quite fond of Darryl. Charley and Wanda kept popping in and we tried to figure out what it could be. We had no clue. He had seemed completely himself on Friday night. What could have happened so suddenly? Charley said he'd better come back. "He owes me twenty bucks."

After lunch I was again on the phone with the pompous ass at Dagner, Smithfield. Mitchell had told me not to concede the last point, so we were off to a roaring start. I was standing at the window looking down at the traffic as we talked. Buses and cars. Gridlock seemed imminent even with the strike settled.

It was then that we heard the second shock. Or squeak. Loretta was squeak/bellowing, "You can't go in there. Wait and I'll ask Mr. Mitchell." Then loud banging and a crash and Loretta calling, "Mr. Mitchell! Mr. Mitchell!"

I told Dagner, Smithfield to hang on, and ran out into the hall in time to see two figures retreat out Darryl's door and disappear into the elevator. Loretta soon appeared, followed by Mitchell and all the secretaries from this side of the floor. The receptionist had come back, all aflutter, spreading the word, in confidence, of course, that they were cops and they had refused to wait. She said with a laugh that she had asked them for a search warrant.

Loretta, having regained her composure, was more self-important than ever for the rest of the afternoon as she recounted and recounted the way they had banged open the door of Darryl's office and wouldn't believe at first that he was not there. Loretta said they were FBI, but the receptionist insisted they were New York cops. Someone said they were fake cops. Hit men.

The partners never told us a thing, of course, if they knew, although they were very much interested in hearing about our dealings with Darryl. In our own minds, we were confident that he was lying on the beach in Haiti. Wanda reluctantly agreed he was probably with the man friend. We speculated endlessly about his past. Wanda thought he was in the witness relocation program. I though he was harboring a fugitive. Charley, thinking of his twenty dollars, said he was probably a con man. I heard Darryl's voice: "OPM" he had said.

Darryl's office remained dark for more than a month. Then one day a funny little red-headed guy moved in, filling the office with familiar sounds of corporate law.

On the first anniversary of Darryl's disappearance, Wanda and Charley and I held the first annual Darryl Hilton Memorial Haitian Ball, which, Wanda pointed out, did not include Darryl Hilton, was, as far as we knew, not memorial, and was not a ball. We did though hold it at a Haitian restaurant, the only one we could find, a dismal place in Brooklyn. About then I found where they were storing Darryl's stuff on the twenty-ninth floor, and took the Munch lithograph or print or whatever it really was to hang in my office.

Last year, we decided to hell with a strict verisimilitude and went to a fine Brazilian restaurant on Fifty-Seventh Street. As we toasted Darryl, Charley took out his pocket calculator and figured the accumulated interest on Darryl's twenty-dollar loan, at a floating rate tied to prime. Wanda suggested that Charley write it off as a bad debt on his tax return, but Charley said, no, he was patient.

We came back to the Brazilian place this year, today. It looks like it is a full-fledged tradition after three years now. Charley even came from downtown. He left the firm last year and went to Manny Hanny's legal department. He maintains, in that pompous voice of his, that it was an offer too good to let go. Wanda and I think he got the axe in his last review. Wanda had a very promising series of dates last spring. She thought this guy was the one. But when she wouldn't let him do quite what he wanted to do after a sixth date, she never heard from him again. I'm still at the grind; never did pull the cord. Actually I was lucky to get away for the dinner. We are in the middle of a tender offer and I've barely slept in a week.

After dessert, Wanda and Charley and I drank another toast to Darryl down on the beach in Haiti with his boyfriend, and Wanda added she hoped he hasn't picked up that scary new disease, AIDS. AIDS — which has replaced gridlock as number one topic of conversation in the city — is probably the only thing new since Darryl left; oh, and Abby made partner, but no surprise there. Interest rates are down, of course. Charley was lamenting that. He did less well this year on his accrual of interest on the debt. After a last toast, I said goodbye and left them. I had to go back to the office to work on the tender offer.

Abigail At Play

"**L**ET ME SEE, JAMIE."

"Not much of a fortune," I said, handing it to her. "I'm going to have many children, it seems."

"Maybe you started the first one last night."

"Ya think?"

"More likely this morning," she said, with a little too much thought and confidence.

"Maybe the first one is out there somewhere, all grown up," I mused.

"I wouldn't be surprised."

I was with Abigail, having a latish dinner at Hunan Balcony on Ninety-eighth Street. She was regaling me with stories about people at her law firm, a fuck-up named Charley she had been forced to use on a recent project, and a guy named Darryl who had come and gone quickly. She was glad to see him go because she thought he might be serious competition for a partnership slot. She was more and more focused on making partner these days. She had told me the Darryl story already, so now I told her we were getting like old married people repeating stories. Well, we were certainly not like old married people.

We had spent our typical Saturday in bed, and when we both realized at the same moment we were famished, rushed out to eat without bothering even to shower. We reeked of sex, but what the hell, it was the weekend. And who would notice in the olfactory banquet of a Chinese restaurant. Abigail's hand was sliding up my leg under the table. Maybe we weren't done yet. I raised my eyebrows.

"Later," she said.

As we cracked open a second set of fortune cookies and wondered what to do next, I looked at my watch and saw it was a little before intermission time down on Broadway. Broadway the place, that is. We were already on Broadway the street.

"Let's go see a show," I said.

"Which one?" she asked. We'd seen quite a few good endings lately.

"I don't know. Let's try *Amadeus*."

"Yeah, I've been wanting to see that." She gave me a dirty look because I had gone to see the whole play when she was in Minnesota visiting her grandmother.

"The beginning was — pretty neat," I said. Kind of silly to rub it in, but what can I say? I couldn't help myself.

She gave me a look well beyond dirty.

I glanced at my watch again, and said, "We better rush."

We quick timed to Ninety-sixth Street. The subway would be way faster than a taxi. I plunked two tokens into the slot and we hurried down the stairs. I was hoping for a two or three train, but a one came. We looked at each other and shrugged. With the local it would be tight. But better to hop on than wait. Maybe an express would catch us at Seventy-second Street.

As we sat on the train, I stated my annoyance at the molded seats in the new cars. Instead of the long, flat benches, some imbecile designer had scooped out individual seats on the plastic bench. They were so narrow you ended up sitting on the pointed edge if anyone at all was sitting next to you. Mayor Koch's fat ass sure wouldn't fit in those seats.

"Who's repeating himself like an old married person now?" Abigail said, having heard it enough times before.

Seventy-second Street came and went. No waiting express train. We sat fretting as the stations clacked by. When the doors finally opened at Times Square, Abigail yanked me up. "Come on, Jamie, let's go."

We climbed the steps, and she asked, "Which theater is it?"

I stopped short. "I don't remember," I said, with a little laugh. I scanned the scene before us, trying to get my bearings.

"Jamie, you idiot."

"Let's try Forty-fourth Street," I said as we hurried along.

"There it is," Abigail said, pointing. "The Broadhurst." The intermission crowd was milling around out front, smoking, some with drinks in their hands. We were good. We slowed down. Abigail stopped, so I stopped. She looked at me up and down and then scrunched her chin against her neck looking at herself. "What were we thinking?" she asked. "We're dressed like shit. We're going to really stand out."

"It'll be fine," I reassured her, looking down at myself, and actually not really so sure. I was wearing a wrinkled denim shirt and frayed jeans. Abigail was usually impeccably dressed. In fact, my casual attitudes toward dress and social behavior in general seemed to bother her more and more as she rose through the ranks at her law firm. But tonight she had thrown on an old sweater she kept at my apartment for chilly nights. She had forgotten it was pretty ratty, all out of shape and actually had holes in it. I mean, we had just popped out for a quick dinner. Who knew we were headed for a Broadway show?

She looked at me. I shrugged, and we walked on.

We loitered in the outer lobby, playing at making small talk and laughing with gusto. A few well-appointed women gave us a once-over. A couple of men smoking pipes gave Abigail more than a once-over as their wives chatted. People were starting to crush out their cigarettes, some on the marble floor, others in the sand tray on top of the waste can, and drift back in. It was time. We both took deep breaths at the same moment, saw it and laughed at each other. Forced ourselves to put on assured looks, and plunged ahead. We followed the crowd in, but then hung back to see who sat where.

An usher on the other side of the door eyed us. I nodded to him. Abigail smiled. He returned the barest modicum of a nod as we passed.

"Balcony or main?" she asked, as we walked. "We need to be decisive."

Abigail was risk averse, but I wanted to go for a good seat.

"See that old lady up front?"

"We're not going to get anything that close," Abigail said. "Let's start from the back."

"No, I feel like the old lady is by herself."

"Which old lady? They're everywhere."

"One, two, three, fifth row, right in the center, with the pale green dress. And you see next to her, three empty."

"I don't know. How likely? The people probably just haven't gotten back to their seats yet."

"Ask. Put on your innocent look and do it," I said urgently as the lights were blinking again.

We walked down the aisle. I winked at a woman standing in front of her seat frowning at us.

We reached the fifth row. Practically on the stage. So conspicuous. What *were* we thinking? Abigail bent down toward the woman in the green dress, batted those blue eyes and smiled. "Excuse me, is anyone in these seats? We have a pretty bad view from where we are."

The woman looked up. Her freshly-done hair was some shade of brown, but not quite right, a touch too much red that made it slightly unnatural. Her deep-set eyes, the lashes heavily mascaraed, gave us a sharp appraising look. "I'm sorry to say, they are taken, dear. My daughter and two grandchildren." She pursed her very red lips, in the briefest smile of finality and dismissal. Her eyes couldn't help drifting over us once more. "I'm sure," she added, her eyes returning to Abigail's, "you'll be quite fine wherever you belong."

My hotshot corporate-lawyer girlfriend sagged noticeably as the woman held her gaze.

"No one in these two." A grizzled old codger in the fourth row cranked his neck back, pointed, and removed his sweater from the seat next to him."

"Oh, thanks so much," Abigail gushed.

We hurried to sit down and squeezed each other's hands as the theater started to darken.

"Always good to see young people at the theater," our benefactor said in his hoarse voice. "Gives answer to Paul Simon's question, no?"

Leaning forward to see him over Abigail, I peered at him somewhat confused.

"Whether or not the theater is dead," Abigail said, staring at me like I was a moron.

"That's it, honey. That's it exactly."

Paul Simon didn't say that, I thought. Some tedious bore he was painting as pathetic said it. Not worth the effort of mentioning. Instead I rolled my eyes; the least I could do to maintain my dignity. Abigail was too busy chatting up her new friend to notice.

I sat back, ready to enjoy the rerun; rerun for me anyway. The second half of the show commenced.

We were close enough to see sprays of spittle. Salieri was a different actor from when I had come before, but Mozart was the same. I liked the former Salieri better. I whispered that to Abigail. Not the smartest tactical move. She gave me a viciously dirty look, but she did not find the gesture fully satisfactory, fully expressive of her annoyance. So she gave my balls such a quick, hard squeeze that I jerked up in my seat and had all I could do to keep from crying out. This cruel indignity beset me at a rather solemn moment in the drama on stage, but Abigail, fourth row center, practically in the laps of the actors, sat there shaking with laughter.

When Elsa Sang The Blues

E LSA DIDN'T KNOW ME from Adam in the early years, but that didn't matter. She was always there for me, providing much needed balm in the smoky dark. By now, on this hot July night, she did know me. I didn't think she knew my name though. I was just "Honey," as in when I walked up and sat down on a stool and she was in the middle of a song, she would see me and interrupt herself to say, "How you tonight, Honey?" or "I missed you last week, Honey." And if she was not in the middle of a song at the moment, she might stand her corpulent body in its glittery pants suit up from her piano seat, reach over the bar and give me a welcoming hug.

"Elsa," I said. "I came in Thursday last week and you weren't here. Paulie said you don't play Thursday now."

"No, I don't play Thursdays no more."

"Really? Since when?"

"Oh, long time now. Where you been, Honey?"

"I've been here some, just mostly Fridays," I said defensively, looking around for Trudy. I could rarely stay out till the wee hours on weekdays, and recently I had not been free on weekends either.

"No, I don't play Thursday. Not for a year or more." Elsa was starting to tap at the piano.

"Why?" I said. Even if I couldn't come, I expected the option to be there.

"Too much. Too much," she said, shaking her head vehemently. The desultory melody took shape, as Debby, the bass player, Malcolm, the drummer, the semi-regular bongo player and a sit-in sax player followed her. She bent into the mic, and sang her signature song, "I Got A Right To Sing The Blues."

Trudy, weaving in and out among the tangle of bodies, plunked my bottle of beer onto the bar and slapped down a napkin. "I'll run a tab," she said over her shoulder, her curls bobbing, as she disappeared into the crowd. I sat back and sipped my beer, settling into the fog of cigarette smoke, the plinking piano, and Elsa's melted-butter voice, as a music critic had described it several years before.

"Thursday was always the best night. Just you." I pressed my case when the song was over and the clapping died down. "And not so clogged up with college kids and bridge people."

She was already playing the first bars of "Stormy Weather."

"The bridge and tunnel people tip well," she said. "Some of them anyway."

"I remember when it used to be just you *every night*, Thursday, Friday, and Saturday. Just you and the piano, all night long."

She stopped playing, looked over at me, thought for a moment and said, "Oh that was years ago."

"Yeah."

"You been coming here that long, Honey?"

"Yeah."

"Oh Lord, Honey, time you get you a woman and settle down." She laughed her big throaty laugh, her jowls shaking.

"Yeah."

Elsa had second thoughts and started playing a different tune. When she leaned into the mic, she said, "This is for my friend Jamie. He been coming here too long." She laughed into the mic and started singing "Blue Moon."

All I could do was shake my head in wonder and let out a quiet laugh. Jamie indeed. I took a last swig of my beer, and got Trudy's attention for another.

The old man next to me had heard our conversation. "You don't have a woman," he reflected with slurred words. Thas a pity. Pity." He went back to his silent communion with his beer.

"You?" I said, in a bit of a mocking tone. I was far from in the best of moods.

"Yeah, right," he mumbled to his beer and then looked over at Elsa. "She's my girl, Elsa's my girl, God love her."

We were sitting at the back of the narrow saloon, around a rectangular bar that surrounded the musicians on three sides. The main bar and a row of small tables stretched toward the entrance. In the corner of my eye I saw a back-lit shape in the distance open the entrance door, hair blowing outward. My heart thudded an extra beat. I looked away and took another swig of my beer, aware suddenly that I had started shaking one leg up and down on the bar stool so that it vibrated. Too much time passed. I looked again. Nobody heading my way. A woman was talking with the bartender, the fan above now blowing her hair. I looked at my watch. Why was I kidding myself? I knew Abigail would not come.

Half an hour later, the old man stood abruptly, banged a five into the fishbowl on top of the piano with an unsteady hand — "Thank you Harry. You take care." — grunted a farewell to Elsa and shuffled out.

I nodded in his direction, feeling remorse for my mean-spirited response to him. He didn't see.

I glanced at the now empty seat beside me. I was not always here alone. I closed my eyes and peopled that seat with ghosts. When I opened my eyes, the seat was filled by a woman who took a few moments to settle her bulk in. A man's hand rested on her shoulder from behind. I took another sip of my beer. Curious, I stole a quick direct look. She noticed. She turned to me. Her eyes were sparkling green. She smiled. It took me aback. The smile contorted her face in a way that was not becoming, but at the same time something about the eyes and the smile was radiant. "This is our first time here," she offered.

"You're in for a treat," I said. "Elsa is the best. She's unique."

She nodded. "She's great. We've been standing for a while farther back." She smiled again, more intimately. "She sang 'Blue Moon' for you."

I gave a little laugh. I didn't know what to say.

"You know her pretty well."

"I wouldn't say that. I've been coming here a while, that's all."

"She wants you to be happy," she said in a soft, kind voice.

I smiled a little awkward smile. I blurted out shyly, "Like you."

She smiled, hesitated for a moment, then gave a quick little nod. The hand on her shoulder said words to her and she turned the smile to him.

Elsa was launching into something. I drank my beer, reflecting on the women I had brought here; none of whom were offering me radiant smiles this night.

A sad procession of women. Well, not sad when they were sitting there, but it made me sad now. Tammy, I think her name was Tammy. Her name escaped me, but the moment was indelible. Maybe we'd had three or four promising dates. Elsa sang one of those songs meant only for lovers. How could we not kiss to it. Quite intensely, as it developed. Then the moment was diverted by the colossally unromantic vision of Donald, his round face and big white teeth inches from our mouths — really, at most three inches — cackling merrily. "Tongue sandwich," he screeched. The merry bass player died in his fifties, a long time ago.

Tammy had happy tears in her eyes as we walked to the subway arm in arm afterwards. "Such a romantic place." She squeezed my hand, stopped to hug me.

I had thought she was going to last a while. I wanted to be serious about her. She was very serious about me. I thought the night with Elsa had clinched it. Not so, not after a lack of impulse control enabled by booze at a party with her close friends. I was out on the balcony trailing after her married friend so obviously that all her friends could not help but be aware of it. Tammy was hurt, deeply embarrassed, and when she broke up with me two days later, she cried. She said she was crying for me, my inability to feel. Well, I do feel.

I checked my watch again, glanced at the door. Elsa was drifting into the hot songs. "Kitchen Man" right now. He was heating up her griddle to the great raucous enjoyment of the crowd. I threw in a "Yeah Elsa," though I didn't feel it.

Abigail and I had fun together. Didn't that count for something? We really had fun.

I thought back to another woman who had sat beside me. Robin. I still wonder from time to time where Robin is now, what her life is like. There was no part of my relationship with Robin that was not intense. The sex was filthy, all-consuming. Our fights were monumental.

New Year's Eve, whatever year it was, we were coming here. Paulie never takes reservations, even for New Year's Eve, but there is an occupancy limit. So first come, first served. If we didn't get moving we would not get in. I was pushing her and pushing her, but she was taking forever. Plus she had a bout of nausea just as we were walking out the door. We were not exactly in a festive mood by the time we rushed off the subway, me dragging her so she practically had to run to keep up in her high heels.

Paulie was at the door along with a big sign that said "Couples Only." I found that quite upsetting. The principle of it offended me. What if I had been alone? I couldn't welcome in the New Year with Elsa? He said, "I don't want the place erupting in fights. Couples keeps things more peaceful." He placed his big hand on my shoulder. "You I would let in. Elsa would never forgive me if I didn't." Not the point, I thought. Robin was yanking me in.

The joint was shaking and it was not yet ten o'clock. It goes without saying, there were no longer any seats. Elsa waved; I steered us through to her, and she hugged me. Hugged us both. New balloons were up along with all the decorations for all the other holidays that never got taken down. We relaxed soon enough into the festive atmosphere. Robin was secure now in our decision, her decision; secure enough that she drank. A lot.

The waitress was giving out hats, noisemakers. At midnight, we all blew and pulled down balloons and batted them around the bar while Elsa sang "Auld Lang Syne." Robin blew her noise-maker in my ear and batted me on the head with a balloon. We kissed. Robin was eight weeks pregnant. After the abortion, somehow, things were never quite the same. I loved her. "Not enough to make a commitment," she had told me firmly.

So much past. Abigail, Abigail. My shoulders fell inward and my head sank.

"Elsa," I said, trying to perk myself up. "Play 'Stick It Where You Stuck It Last Night.'"

Elsa barely shook her head. "Ain't nobody's birthday."

Ah yes. Had to be for a birthday or an engagement. The reason was obscure. Once upon a night, I was alone and struck up a conversation with the woman next to me. She was with her boyfriend but was happy enough to chat with me. That would have driven me crazy if I were the boyfriend. We talked about the array of hot songs we had heard Elsa sing over the years, laughing together as we each came up with a more obscure one, and came eventually to that one. We whispered strategy. "Hey Elsa," I said. "It's his birthday," pointing.

"No it's not," Elsa said.

"It is," the woman lied.

"Come on, Elsa, play it."

To our consternation, she broke into the first bars of "Happy Birthday."

"Nooo," I said.

"What's his name?" Elsa asked the woman.

"Pat."

"Pat?'

"Pat."

"We gonna sing happy birthday to Pat, everyone."

And they all did, while I whined, "That's not what we wanted, Elsa. You know that."

"Well that's all you're getting."

After the applause ended, I repeated, "You know what we want, Elsa."

And the woman echoed my words. Someone down the bar shouted encouragement.

Donald led the boys in the band in playing the first bars. She relented without changing her frowning expression or saying a word.

"There was a boy who loved a girl."

"Yeah," I said as the woman and I clapped. And so the "verses" flowed, most of them made up on the spot. "...Pat put sand in the Vaseline."

By the final refrain, just about everyone in the bar was joining in, singing out the title, "Stick It Where You Stuck It Last Night," and Elsa was calling people out for solos. "The lady in the polka dots." In a quavering voice. "My drummer." Shouting and banging on the drums. "Trudy, there." Belting it out as she placed two beers. "Even the bartender." A loud baritone from off in the front. "One more time, everybody now." Applause, laughter, silence.

"Thank you Elsa," I said. The woman, the girlfriend, thanked her too. Pat did not.

I turned and wished Pat a happy birthday. The woman gave a quiet little laugh. Pat did not.

At some point, I slipped the woman my phone number. She gave me a look. Then she gave me the faintest of smiles and slid the scrap of napkin into her purse. But she never called. I had felt as if she and I hit it off. But I guess I couldn't compete with the birthday boy.

I sure hit it off with Abigail. I thought *we* hit it off.

I looked at the door and checked my watch. Now it was late. Too late.

When I say they had all sat next to me at the bar, that is not quite true. Abigail never came with me, never once. Abigail was most of the reason I had not been there much recently. She knew how much I loved the place. You would think she would want to share it with me, at least try. "I don't do scuzzy bars reeking of cheap beer and festooned" — she paused to give me a look — "with drunken morons." This she had said the first and only time I proposed we head for Elsa on a Saturday night. And of course her characterization wasn't far off. I looked around at the crowd. An inebriated college idiot was screaming "Yeah Elsa," and letting out drunken whoops. Elsa was singing "Long John" and the frat boy repeated every line after her, and when she sang about his six foot height, he screamed "how tall?" Yeah, not Abigail's kind of place.

I was no college boy anymore. Soon I was going to be entering the frightening fourth decade of my life, or I guess it is the fifth. The one in which the birthdays start with the number four. My God that was an ominous number coming up. I wondered what Abigail had been planning to get me.

Elsa played her intermission song and stood up. A relative silence fell over the saloon. I looked up, scanned the people around the bar, including several quite cute women. I had not even noticed them. That was so not the pre-Abigail me, not even to notice.

At a small table near my stool sat a pretty young woman, wearing a business suit and bow tie. She looked tired, and her face was expressionless. I gazed at her; she noticed nothing. She daydreamed mostly, her cheek squashed down against her hand. After a while she was joined by a young lawyer, accountant, whatever he was. She looked up, without expression, as he reached into a paper bag and plunked down, one after another, packages of dental floss. "I didn't know what kind you wanted," he said. She smiled silently and took his hand. She kissed it, and nuzzled it against her cheek. That gesture brought back a long ago picture of a woman named Daphne. I found myself lost in memories when Elsa returned to the crash of drums and patter of bongos.

The chair next to me grated against the floor as someone pulled it out and sat down. I glanced over. A guy around my age. He nodded. I nodded back and looked away. Didn't want to appear too friendly. But he pushed. Held out his hand. "Nicky," he said. I reluctantly touched his hand and said "Jamie."

"I think I've seen you here. You look familiar."

"Maybe. I'm not here as much as I was."

"Yeah, me either. I liked to come on Thursdays. Much mellower, purer if you know what I mean."

"I know exactly what you mean," I said, feeling my outrage return.

"But now she doesn't play Thursdays."

"Hey Elsa," I called, "He wants you to come back on Thursdays too."

She peered over at us, squinting to see who he was. She recognized him and nodded briefly.

"Not happening," she snapped.

"Buy you a beer?" he said.

"No thanks." I looked at him. Awkward moment. I decided he wasn't putting moves on me, just needed to talk to someone. I said, "What do you do?" Such a stupid question, but something to say.

"Lawyer."

"Uhh." I started to say my girlfriend is a lawyer, but then that wasn't true now, was it? Her being my girlfriend. As of tonight! As of about six hours ago.

"You?" he asked.

"I teach."

"High school?"

"No, I'm up at the university."

"Nice. Professor? Sure I can't get you a beer?"

"Indeed I am. No, I'm good." I touched my beer.

"Good? Ha, *I'm* not good. Not a good night. Not a good fortnight." I did a double-take at that unexpected word. No trace of irony in his expression; just unhappiness.

"Tell me about it!" I agreed heartily.

"You ever get dumped by a teenager?" Well, this night was getting bizarre fast, I thought.

"Not recently." I said. "How about by the most perfect woman I ever knew? Like tonight, for instance. The one I thought was going to be forever."

"Sorry."

"Yeah, well."

He said, "I've had a couple of weeks to get used to it; I guess I mean stew in it."

"Indeed, a fortnight."

"I can't. Can't even begin to get used to it. I mean, age doesn't matter, God damn it. We belong together. It's so fucked. Timing. Timing determines everything. If Ecaterina and I were both ten years older, the age thing just wouldn't have scared her so much. Timing. She said I have experienced things; everything is new to her. She needs someone to grow with her. I could have said, 'or grow away from you.'"

I grunted agreement.

"Cat's diabetic," he blurted out. "The really bad kind."

"Bummer."

"I want to be there for her when she needs someone. I want to take care of her."

"Yeah well, wrong timing, as you said. Apparently she doesn't want someone who wants to take care of her. She sounds like right now she wants to be independent."

"Yeah, and when she realizes she needs someone, she'll discover she already met that someone..."

"At the wrong time," I said.

Timing. I timed out with Abigail. I reached my expiration date.

"What happened with you and your woman?" Nicky asked. "Big fight?"

"Abigail doesn't fight. She asserts. I don't much have a say in her truth."

"Abigail? That's her name?" Nicky said.

"Yeah, Abigail."

He stared at me. "What?" I asked.

He shook his head, and said, "Go on." But then he said, "I was just thinking, Abigail's kind of an unusual name these days."

"I guess. I never thought about it really. She is Abigail. Abigail is she. Inextricable."

"I'm picturing her tall, thin, with long auburn hair."

I nodded. "You're psychic."

"You said she's a lawyer, right?"

"I don't think I did say, but she is."

"Does she ever call herself Abby?"

"No. She doesn't like that at all."

Nicky smiled, nodded, said, more to himself than me, "Life is stranger than fiction."

"Huh?

"Nothing. Go on with what you were saying."

"I was saying, there was no issue. No discussion. She just told me I no longer fit her requisites. That was the word she used. I didn't fit her professional needs. One day we were in bed all day, crashing a Broadway show at night; then suddenly goodbye. 'But we had a lot of fun, kid. I'll cherish that.' You believe she actually said that?"

"Oh, yes, I believe it."

"I was not quite *appropriate* at this point in her career, she said."

Nicky flared in anger. "Appropriate. I never want to hear that word again. Cat used that word. Not appropriate for her to be with someone my age. Fucking women. Your girlfriend is a real shit, uh, sounds like a real shit. You're better off without her."

"I was so sure she was the one. I've been sitting here wallowing, thinking about past women, *a la recherché de femme perdu*, as it were. The stupid ways I blew it. Indulging self-revulsion, if you must know. But let me tell you, I didn't blow it with Abigail. I worshiped her."

"What is it?" he asked, seeing the pained expression that had come over my face.

"I can't believe I used the past tense. I worship her. I always will. Present tense, future tense."

"Always is a long time."

"You know who is a shit?" I said. "M-E, me. Do you ever have moments when you're suddenly overwhelmed with guilt for things that happened so long ago it's as if they didn't really happen? Then they pop into your head. Things that make you cringe, make you loathe yourself? You want to hear a story?"

"Sure, what do I have but time now? Time and beer."

"So you tell me who's a shit. This story is from a long time ago, back when I was in graduate school. Daphne, that was the name of the shitee. All night I have had a picture in my head of Daphne.

"The last time I ran into her, we were both doing our laundry in the local laundromat. About half a year after we had stopped seeing each other. She told me she was getting married. I said that was nice. Anyhow, I helped her fold a sheet."

"I assume you had dumped her."

"Dump implies something fast and sudden. Daphne went very slowly. Well, whatever; there she was. Warm and close. As I gave her my end of the sheet, I kissed her, gently. I still remember the roughness of her cracked lips and the moist warmth of her breath. She kissed me back. Then she stood there looking sad. She said her shrink told her I expressed the rage that she repressed."

"Woopy doo for shrinks. Profound. I'm sure they would have all kinds of sick reasons I was with a nineteen year old." He snatched up his beer and downed half the bottle.

"No one could say I had not been utterly straight with Daphne, but she loved me. She told me I loved her. She told me it was just my defenses that made me so cold. I told her I knew quite definitely that I didn't love her. I had a friend of ours named Edie tell her I didn't love her."

"She didn't accept it?"

"No, *she* knew better. One day Edie gave a party and Daphne waltzed in, knowing I would be there. When Edie saw Daphne, she high-stepped over to her and without even a hello told her not to go home with me. She said it with such intense abruptness that it was funny and they both laughed. I saw the laughter from a sunken sofa. As for the words, Edie reported them soon enough, in a tone of voice laden with threat and accusation.

"As the party ran its course, I stayed across the room from Daphne. I was sipping a Rolling Rock and listening with a few other people to Edie and this professor named Ronald talk. Ronald had a lofty reputation in academic circles. He was always perfectly groomed and dressed, polite and charming in conversation, never ruffled, always a gently remote glossy surface. Edie was pretty and slight, and spoke carefully, but with intensity. Visualize the two of them politely conversing, the others straining to hear Edie. Such a very academic moment. I picked up a strand of the conversation. Ronald took a pretzel and focused on me, nodding as I spoke.

"I felt the intrusion of a hand abruptly massaging my back. I knew it was Daphne. It could only be. I shook her off. In the awkward silence that came over the group, Daphne turned to Ronald — that facade of remote gentility — and said, 'He's really very sensitive. He just has this need to keep up a front.' Ronald's face was a twinkling mask as always. Edie frowned at Daphne, and, wide-eyed, glared at me as I turned to face Daphne."

Trudy bustled over, curls bobbing. She nodded to someone across the bar who was waving for her and holding up two fingers. She looked at us. "How you guys doing?"

Nicky dipped his head at me. I shook mine. "I'll have another," he said.

Trudy sashayed off. "I love her curls," I said.

"Yeah, nice. How old you think she is?"

I thought about it. "Forty-five maybe, give or take. Why, you thinking of going the other way on the age scale?"

"Not really, I guess."

"Well, it's a positive sign that you gave her a look at least."

He didn't respond. Then he said, "So get back to Daphne. I know something is coming."

"Ah, that it is. So let's see. She came out with that cringe-worthy statement. I just stared for a moment into her round, brown eyes. She looked placid, beatific, having claimed me, publicly, there in that collegial forum. The Rolling Rock I held was still half full."

"Oh," he said. I raised my eyebrows. "Go on," he urged.

"She saw what was coming, but she stood there passively.

"I demonstrated that her statement concerning my sensitivity was inaccurate. As I held the tipped bottle steady over her head, our eyes were locked and I could see myself, as in a fun house, in her pupils. The foam rolled down her cheeks, and rivulets veered to the corners of her mouth, and dripped on down. When the bottle was empty, I turned back. I handed the bottle to Edie and asked her for another beer. Her disgust was all facial. She said nothing. Ronald's lips pressed tight, his eyes sparkled away as I proceeded to finish my point. Daphne dried herself off with napkins Edie brought her."

"They didn't kick you out?"

"No, we were all pretty close friends, except for Ronald of course. Later, only several of Edie's friends remained. Smoke clung to the curtains and a mellow late-night coziness settled over the darkened room. A murmur of voices; scattered plates and ashtrays, empty bottles. You know, that mellow after-party feel. Edie, Daphne and some others were cleaning up."

"Why do I know what's coming?"

"Yeah, well, my eyes were following Daphne as she came and went with plates and cups and napkins. She saw me watching and I believe we both knew right then what you know. When she later put on her coat, I quietly got mine. Edie stood, with a dish towel in her hand, seething."

As I spoke, I could hear Elsa singing "Body and Soul"; just her and her piano, slow and soft. Oh yes, Daphne was there for me, every bit of her. Anything I wanted, mine. But I didn't want it. I sometimes ponder why. She was very desirable. A lot of guys tried. "I was sure hot for her, but I didn't want her. Maybe I should have wanted her."

"You can't force yourself, you just can't. It is all so...mysterious, I guess. That's the thing, Cat and I had it; it was so utterly clear that we did. It is so fucked."

"Timing."

"Yeah."

"That night the timing was right for Daphne and me," I said. "We could barely wait. Pretty sick, huh?"

"Go on," he said.

"Flung our clothes off. I slapped her ass hard. She cried out. Lay there quite still, waiting. I turned her over and her arms came up to pull me to her. I remember I smelled the beer in her hair as she groaned under me. Beads of sweat formed over her lip and her eyeballs darted under her closed lids. Her forehead twisted with frowns and her cheeks puckered as she exploded into — into fulfillment.

"'You see?' she said. She had her chin on her palm and she was smiling at me. She kissed my hand and nuzzled her face into it."

"You're a shit," Nicky said.

"A sensitive shit, if truth be told. Daphne was correct."

We were silent for a time. I turned toward Elsa. "Elsa, we need a really sad song. Make us cry, Elsa. I think we need to cry."

She frowned at me. Glanced at Nicky. Back at me. But she obliged. Played "Cry Me A River." It didn't much matter what she chose. We cried. We did.

Elsa peered at us. Her fingers paused over the keys. "Stop that now. Two grown men. My Lord."

"You've got a talent there, Elsa," a woman said.

"I don't want no talent like that. No way."

I looked over at Nicky. "I feel like we're just two losers reciting our sad tales. Like what that crooner used to call a saloon song."

Nicky wiped his eyes with a napkin. "Pathetic."

"All the opportunities I chose not to take. Chose."

"Yeah." Nicky looked at his watch. "Damn, I have to go into the office tomorrow, early, believe it or not; I'm working on a deal with Ab — with another lawyer. It's been nice talking. I'm sure I'll see you again."

I nodded.

Nicky stood up. He stared at me for a few seconds. "Ponder this," he said. "The woman you finally did choose is truly a shit. A heartless shit." He turned and walked out.

Elsa gave me a look, shook her head. She played "Mood Indigo"; didn't sing it.

I sat there staring at my beer, focusing on details, the sweating on the tinted glass, a little droplet rolling down. The label slightly peeled. I twisted the bottle around with my fingers as the music played. I tested the label, pulling at it. It came a little looser. I saw Daphne's face, her eyes. I saw Abigail. Was she a heartless shit? Saw Daphne. Was I? I twisted the beer again, trying to twist Daphne away. But her presence hung in the air, her warmth, her smell, her taste. And then I picked the bottle up and poured it over my head.

"What are you doing. You stop that right now." I became aware of Elsa glaring at me. She had ceased playing. "My land."

I set the bottle down. My shirt felt cold and soggy. I shivered. My neck felt like goose bumps.

"Trudy, bring this man a towel. What were you thinking? What in God's name were you thinking?"

I wiped my hair with the towel Trudy handed me as she rushed by with three beers somehow clinging to her other hand. Elsa went back to playing the piano, shaking her head. I sat.

At three a.m. I wandered out to the strains of the Gershwin song, "But Not For Me."

"You take care now, Honey, you hear me?"

"See you, Elsa. You too." I dropped a twenty into the bowl. I don't know why I had been looking at the door all night. Futile hope, that is why. Because she knew exactly where I would go, even if she had never been here. She knew it as surely as I knew she wouldn't come. I sighed a big sigh as I walked toward the front.

The tourists and bridge people were long gone. Most of the regulars too. Only a few seats were occupied. Sodden heads rested on palms held up by elbows. One couple clung to each other practically in the same seat. I pushed open the door, and found Paulie out front in the summer night, the strangely silent, fresh night after the beery cacophony of the bar.

"It makes me sad," I said to him.

"What does?" he asked, humoring the slightly intoxicated patron. For a tall, husky, imposing man, Paulie was unexpectedly soft-spoken. He gave my wet shirt a quick glance.

"That Elsa doesn't play on Thursdays." My voice rose in hurt.

"What can I do?" he said, raising his hands palms up. "She doesn't want to work anymore."

"It's not the same," I said.

"She doesn't want to work," he repeated earnestly. "Only a matter of time now." He ran a hand through his slicked back graying hair. "It's her decision." We looked at each other, each of us considering the import of that. "What you learn in this business," he went on, "is that no one is indispensable."

The words gave me a sick feeling. I wanted to ask him if that was also true in life.

"When she's not here, it's pretty empty." It was a halfhearted, resigned response.

"I know. You don't have to tell me."

I had nothing else to say.

"Maybe when she retires, I will too," he said matter-of-factly.

We were quiet for a time, just gazing at each other.

"I'll sell the place," he called after me as I walked away down the sidewalk.

I pondered the inconceivables ricocheting through my head as I wandered off to the Christopher Street/Sheridan Square Station. Down below, the thick heat radiated through the empty tunnel. I heard in my head the piano banging and the voice oozing the heartache of "Body And Soul."

Two express trains clattered by, one after another. Garish designs in spray paint overlapped on the gray metal cars, selfishly, chaotically, devouring the train. The silence afterward was more penetrating for the intrusion.

I found myself once again reliving that distant New Year's Eve with Robin. Elsa singing Guy Lombardo; a joyous jumble of hands pulling balloons from above and batting them here and there. The balloons eased gently through the air, a myriad of brightly-colored globes dancing in the dark until other hands sent them on across the bar, the tables, the piano. Elsa laughed so her entire body jiggled.

When we had reached the station afterwards, still wearing our party hats and blowing on our noisemakers, there stood a welcoming committee of inebriated teenage girls, wishing all and sundry a happy new year as the turnstile clanked. Passing through, we shook their hands, blew our noisemakers at them, at each other, at a passing express train.

When Robin realized she had left her scarf, we stood for a moment debating whether it was worth missing a train. Then we headed back through the turnstile. The lead girl greeter looked us dead in the eyes. "Year New Happy," she said, as we moved in reverse. "A dollar fifty down the drain."

The man in the booth furrowed his brow, gave us an inquisitive cock of his head. I yelled, "Forgot her scarf," and when we returned, he nodded almost imperceptibly and passed us through the gate with his buzzer. We yelled thanks and happy new year to him, and again to the lead girl greeter and her friends, still there. We had not missed the train.

We rode comfortably on the clackety clackety Number One, as the crowd grew larger and cheerier with each stop. Fourteenth Street and a flood of quilted winter colors flowed in. The conductor through the loudspeaker, "Step lively. Watch the closing doors. Eighteenth is next."

A youngish man who looked all right turned to the elderly woman standing beside him and admonished her sternly, "Madame, you did not watch the door close. You were instructed to watch the door close." She walked to the other end of the car.

A woman with a couple of teeth and a stained raincoat was swigging from a bottle and screaming happy new year in the general direction of the floor. A preppy couple who had not invited her to plop down next to them decided to move across the aisle. It was not lost on the woman, and she thereafter directed her joyous tidings at them in a manner both insolent and incoherent.

Even at Eighteenth, more passengers. Penn Station and a swath of people departed. Times Square and more piled in. The train was packed with pleasantly inebriated celebrants standing against each other. The only remaining seat was at the end of the car where a sodden bum slept alone in a seat for two.

The woman with a couple of teeth was still carrying on. New standees, hearing the woman's menacing tones, peered briefly to see what was up, then quickly lost interest. Only a bag lady. Eventually wearying of her tirade, she stood and swayed her way down the aisle, banging into people unabashedly when they proved to be obstacles, until she reached the end of the car and dumped herself down heavily beside the sleeping bum.

"Wek-up," she bellowed, jabbing him hard in the ribs. "Wek-up and have sumintadrink Happcccncwyar."

His bulging eyes opened slowly a jaundiced shade. He reached out mechanically for the bottle and took a swig, still half stuporous.

"Happeeenewyar," she said again. He mouthed those words back to her.

For the next ten minutes or so, as Robin rested her head on my shoulder, the bag lady directed her chatter at the bum and he listened or appeared to, in his sodden way, and they shared the bottle. A few stops later, Robin nudged me and I looked again.

They were asleep together with their arms around each other, her head nuzzled against his neck.

As we watched them, Robin's hand tightened on my leg and her plaintive voice said, "Oh let's resolve to be nice to each other. Please Jamie. Take care of each other. Promise me."

I did.

About The Author

Lewis Bogaty is a writer and photographer living in New York. *Loves And Entanglements*, his first short story collection, was published in 2024. His fiction has also appeared in *Virginia Quarterly Review*, *Mississippi Review*, *Descant*, *Sou'Wester*, *Another Chicago Magazine*, *Confrontation*, and others. His non-fiction has appeared in *Virginia Quarterly Review, Columbia Law Review,* and various other magazines and newspapers.

His short story in *Kansas Quarterly* received a *Kansas Quarterly*/Kansas Arts Commission fiction award. He has also received a BRIO fiction award from the Bronx Council On The Arts. *Loves And Entanglements*, in an earlier version, was a semi-finalist in the 2021 Elixir Press Fiction Award competition.

His photographs have been exhibited in solo and group shows, most recently in Upstream Gallery's 2024 national juried photography show. His images have appeared in the *New York Times* and other newspapers, magazines and corporate publications. His prints are owned by institutions and private collectors.

He holds a Ph.D. in English and a J.D. law degree, and was an editor on the *Columbia Law Review*.

www.LewisBogaty.com

www.LewisBogatyPhotography.com

Instagram: @lewisbogaty

www.ingramcontent.com/pod-product-compliance
Lightning Source LLC
Chambersburg PA
CBHW020107310726
48970CB00002B/522